MW01232624

PERFECTA SAXONIA

JOHN BROUGHTON

Special thanks go to my dear friend John Bentley for his steadfast and indefatigable support. His content checking and suggestions have made an invaluable contribution to

Perfecta Saxonia.

ANGLO-SAXON PLACE NAMES (in order of appearance in *Perfecta Saxonia*)

Sondwic
West Seax
Kingdom of Alba
Temes
Hamwic
Hrofescaester
Suth Seax
Lundenwic
Mierce
Tame Weorth
Weorgoran-caestre
Lygan
Hamtunscir
Saefern
Defnascir
Wiltunscir
Lunden
Eanulfsbirig
Ledecestre
Wealas
Herefordscir
Dyfed
Rumcofan
Brecenanmere
Deoraby
Eoforwic
Jorvik
Deira
Snotingaham

Glevcaestre
Cyrneceaster
Foirthe fjord
Hymbre
Deneport
Badecanwelle
Caestir
Farndune
Bebbanburgh
Narresford
Nordhamptunescir
Nassaburh
Bernicia
Wealisc
Westwealas
Nametwic
Bathum
Sandwich, Kent
Wessex
Scotland
River Thames
Southampton, Hants.
Rochester, Kent
Sussex
The Port of London
Kingdom of Mercia
Tamworth
Worcester
River Lea
Hampshire
River Severn
Devonshire
Wiltshire

London
St. Neot, Cambs.
Leicester
Wales
Herefordshire
Kingdom in S-W.Wales
Runcorn, Cheshire
Llangorse Lake
Derby
York
York (Viking name)
N-E. Celtic Kingdom
Nottingham
Gloucester
Cirencester
Firth of Forth
River Humber
Davenport, Lancs.
Bakewell, Derbys.
Chester
Farndon, Cheshire
Bamborough, Northumberland
Navisford, Northants.
Northamptonshire
Peterborough, Cambs.
N-E. Celtic Kingdom
Welsh
Cornwall
Nantwich, Cheshire
Bath, Somerset

1

SONDWIC, KENT, 894 AD

My passage from boy to manhood, abrupt and hard, bestowed on me many life lessons. Prime among them that happiness should be held at arm's length in a pair of smithy tongs because, if you try to embrace it, you'll be seared to the bone.

I was entering my sixteenth summer when father gave me the greatest joy of my life up to that point. Unknown to me, he spied me at sword practice, disarming the brute of a smith's son, Flodwig. Just because you stand taller than other boys and your chest is as broad as a yearling bull's doesn't mean your muscles can beat your opponent like an iron bar. Not when the one you are up against is as swift as the bird of that name and as smart as a fox in a monastery hen coop.

Sorrowful as I am, I could not help smiling at his gawping expression when his practice sword went sailing over his head.

Father must have shared in my glee too because that very evening in the great hall, he, the noble Ealdorman Ealhere, called me to him. Assembled there, his thegns and bondsmen looked on as he solemnly presented me with his pride and joy, *Breath Stealer*, his incomparable sword crafted in Frankia. He held out the same weapon that won him and his heirs our land on the banks of the Stour, the river he and his grateful King, Athelstan, sailed up more than two-score years past to destroy the Danish fleet. They captured nine of their dragon-prowed ships and routed the rest at the battle off Bloody Point. Verses sung about that glorious day never tire me.

Now, father incomprehensibly handed the blade to me. My eyes grew as round as the bottoms of two leather ale flasks, and my lips formed a protest. But he said, "My son, Ecgwulf, is the finest swordsman, of his age, I have ever seen." Father's cold, steel-grey stare shifted to seek out the fool spluttering a laugh through his beer and came to rest on the idiot, Flodwig. The blacksmith's son's face flared red, and he feigned a coughing fit to cover his embarrassment.

"Father," I said, "I cannot accept *Breath Stealer*; she's yours forever."

"Nothing is forever, lad, except the life eternal. Remember those words when you go into battle, and meanwhile, obey your father!" His face took on a grave expression, one seldom seen – so unlike his handsome, unvaryingly cheerful face. "Where I'm going, I won't be needing her, God willing. Keep her well-honed and greased, son."

In my childishness and in the panicked thought that my begetter was upping and leaving for another land, I did not understand. A moment's reflection would have told me he would need a weapon if he meant to travel in these troubled times. But in those simple days of certainty, the greatest certitude of all was the reassuring strength of our ealdorman protector.

Three weeks later, the church bell tolled one repetitive

mournful note, my happiness drained away and fled wraithlike in search of wherever his soul had gone. The great heart that loved all the folk in our settlement betrayed him. Yet, he must have known, else why would he have gifted me *Breath Stealer?* The mighty sword hung from my belt, too long for my height, and threatened to trip me as I hurried to the church. And, the reality of my situation did not sweep away the dreamlike trance possessing me. It could only be a bad dream – how could Father be dead? And yet, in vain, moments before, I had touched his neck seeking a pulse.

"Lord Ecgwulf," the priest greeted me.

"What?" I said like a perfect imitation of Flodwig – if not in height and brawn, in stupidity.

Sorrow tempered the smile of Father Godfred. "You are the Ealdorman of Sondwic, my son. May God grant you the strength and wisdom to protect your people."

These words chilled me to the marrow but, at the same time, would stay with me for the rest of my life.

"Amen," I said from the depths of my heart, not suspecting how soon the latter virtue would be needed. The first depended only on my dedication to practice and training.

Arrangements in place with Godfred, I hastened back to comfort Ecgwynn. We were orphans now. Mother died of the ague that reaped half the souls in Sondwic when I had but seven winters behind me. Ecgwynn is truly beautiful, I still see Mother's smiling face in my dozing moments, more winsome than her daughter.

I found Ecgwynn slipping a gold arm ring into place over Father's muscular flesh. Flesh soon to decay in the churchyard. I shuddered. Would that my limbs were iron-hard like his. I had swung his sword in the seclusion of my room and wondered how long my tired arm needed to reach the mettle of a warrior.

JOHN BROUGHTON

What if the Danes raided before summer ended? What use is a mere stripling as Ealdorman?

The arm ring was a prized possession given to Father by the King of the West Seaxa and overlord of Kent. Clever of Ecgwynn to remember! In a rush of love, I stepped over to her, she turned up her tear-streaked face to bestow on me the faintest smile. I knelt beside her and took her into my arms. "I am Ealdorman now," I whispered, "and I will protect you. I swear it!"

She rested her flaxen hair with its golden streaks against my shoulder, her tremble made me hold her tighter.

"You are strong," she sighed, "a man now."

Coming from her, two years my elder, this pleased me beyond words. I loved her like a mother, my oath was true. I would spill my last drop of blood to safeguard Ecgwynn.

It must have been this thought and the advice of Father Godfred that drove me into a frenzy of weapon training as soon as our father was decently buried. Fighting the boys who had grown tired of the beatings I gave them did not satisfy me anymore. They did not stretch me to the limits I sought. But I did not need to order any of the menfolk to leave their daily work. Another surprise awaited me in the shape of my father's friend, Osbald, a battle-hardened warrior. Seeing my frustration at overcoming a youth of a score of winters in less than a hundred heartbeats, he wandered over and picked up the wooden practice sword.

"Lord," he said, "if you fight like that in battle, even a hunchback cripple would open you from there to there." He drew the willow blade down my chest to my groin, I flushed red, pushing him away from me with my shield.

"Let's see if you can do that, Osbald. Or if it will be the other way round?" I said, letting the hot-headedness of youth take over.

4

The warrior turned to my scowling, beaten adversary. "Give me the shield, good fellow, though heaven knows, I won't need it."

This remark and the sneer it elicited fanned the flames of my temper. With a cry, I leapt forward and swung a blow at Osbald's head, which he swatted away with contemptuous ease. I rained strike after strike on him, each one meeting the same effortless parrying until my breath came in gasps.

All of a sudden, from whence I had no inkling, the wooden blade of my opponent struck upwards into my groin and left me writhing on the ground. As the object of mirth of the small gathering drawn to gape at the combat, I wanted to leap up and teach Osbald a lesson, but my nether parts sent a gnawing pain to the pit of my stomach and, instead, I lay groaning.

Osbald raised me to my feet and made me bend over time and again until the aching passed. He also growled at the youths who thought to mock their new Lord, bested before their eyes. "If any of you dog turds wish to show you are better than a heap of stinking shit, take up yon sword and prove it. Else shut your foul mouths." With no takers, he turned back to me, "Ready, Lord?"

"Ready."

Indeed, I was all set to hand him a thrashing, but caution told me not to rush in as before, I circled him. This gained me a grunt of approval. The warrior feinted, I was open to the same attack that had undone me. Osbald was a loyal fellow and withheld the strike. If I can make love with a maid, I must thank him for his mercy.

"See that, Lord Ecgwulf?"

I *had* seen, I am a quick learner.

"Think you can do th—"

He didn't have time to finish and, in truth, he wasn't prepared because he was too busy instructing. That was why he lay on the ground with the same searing pain shooting up his innards.

One thing can be said for the folk of Sondwic, they are loyal and honest. A cheer and a slap on my back made me spin to stare into the face of the smith's son, where I found genuine pleasure without a trace of malice.

"Well done, my Lord," he said, his words were worth more than a bag of silver to me.

"Help him up, Flodwig, you're stronger with me being out of breath."

On his feet, Osbald bent over several times, and when he felt better, he gave me a level look.

"First lesson learnt, Lord, in battle strike when your enemy least expects it." He rubbed his groin and grinned at me. "Your late beloved father asked me to give you lessons in swordsmanship. What say you, Lord? Every day an hour before the sun sets?"

"But at that time, the light is not at its best."

"Which is why I chose that time of day. On the morrow, you can tell me why."

With a wry smile, he flung down the practice sword and hobbled away with an uncomfortable gait caused by the lightning strike delivered with a flick of my wrist. Late in the day suited me. Every day, folk needed me for one reason or another. Yesterday I settled a boundary dispute and another brought by an angry ceorl claiming the miller had given him too little flour for the coin he had paid. In addition, I needed to organise the river patrol. Only few men were devoting time to it, and, quite rightly, they complained the task should be shared by more of them. Keeping a wary eye open for Danish long-ships was in everybody's interest. In fact, I enjoyed sailing whenever I got the opportunity. Father had taken me out with him many times but only in fair weather. Never having faced an angry sea, I couldn't claim to be a sailor. I sighed; so much to do and learn: strength and wisdom, I murmured. How right Father Godfred was – *strength and wisdom* were what I needed – by the Lunden bushel-load.

2

SONDWIC, KENT, 894 AD

A wake to the familiar crowing of the cockerel and you believe it is another ordinary day. But some days are pivotal, inevitably, we face them unawares. Humming softly, I strolled past Ecgwynn's chamber, intent on seeking a fresh raw egg to swallow when a sound halted me. My sister sobbing? I listened, not mistaken, the heart-wrenching sound continued. Whatever troubled her was grievous judging by the lament.

I curbed the impulse to burst into her chamber. Would she welcome comfort? Sweet-natured as she is, when crossed, her tongue can be sharper than the lash of a whip. To be honest, when she lost her temper, the fault, without exception, was mine. Although, on occasions, I was slow to admit as much.

That is why I delayed before raising a fist to hammer at her door. By chance, the appearance of another person overcame my hesitancy. The door swung back to reveal a maid. She started and gasped at the sight of my raised fist. I unclenched it to seize her arm and haul her out of Ecgwynn's room, and, with my free hand, I pulled the door closed.

"What ails your mistress?"

The plaintive wailing, muffled by the oak barrier, continued to clutch at my stomach. The girl did not reply but hung her head.

"I asked you a question, girl!"

The young woman, no more than my age, looked up to meet my fierce stare. She did not hold my gaze but stared over my shoulder, a look of anguish on her face.

"Lord, I am sworn to secrecy."

The words came out little more than a whisper, I heard aright.

"Secrecy?"

At that, she nodded her head fit to shake it off.

"Keeping a pledge is admirable," I smiled at her, but as the wench relaxed, my temper rose, "except there is a problem..." The anxiety returned to her face in an instant, and the little fool made to flee past me.

I have not raised a hand against a woman before, and hope I never will again, but instinct led me to block her escape and push her against the wall. She let out a cry, her darting eyes revealed her fear.

"If it has escaped you, that is my sister in there, *I* am your lord and master!" My fingers closed over the hilt of my hand-seax. I did not mean to use it – I never would – but, in fairness, I intended to scare the wits out of her. Her hand flew to her throat, and she swayed on her feet. For a moment, I dreaded she would faint on me.

"I mean you no harm, Lufe. It is Lufe, isn't it?"

I knew full well her name; we had played together in the mud outside the hall when we were knee-high to our parents. The use of her name calmed her.

"Whatever ails your mistress is my affair. You know I care for her."

The young woman nodded, still mute, but accompanied it

with a weak smile. At last, she spoke.

"Lord, my father taught me a person is only worth her word. How can I betray a confidence?"

In truth, I admired her at that moment, as my own father had told me the same words. It gladdened me that Lufe was Ecgwynn's maid, and I rewarded her with what I hoped was a handsome smile, "It would be unfair to ask such a thing of you. I cannot. Now, be off about your business!"

Away she tripped into the hall as if with a demon on her heels. The sobbing did not abate which wiped the smile off my face.

I plucked up courage and knocked on the door. A moment of silence passed from within, then the reddened eyes of Ecgwynn were staring at me from her tear-streaked face.

"Sister, what ails you?" I asked kindly.

"It is not a good time, Ecgwulf," she sighed, "and yet sooner or later, we must talk else I fear I will lose my mind."

"All your tears cannot bring Father back."

"My tears are not for Father," she looked ashamed, "although I miss him so much. How I wish I might seek his advice here and now!"

This came as a stinging slap in my face.

"I am not as wise as he, but I am here for you, sister."

At these words, she stepped forward and pressed her head against my shoulder. Although nothing to do with her plight, I noted with pleasure I had grown taller than her, in spite of the two years that passed between us.

"If you cannot talk with me," I said through clenched teeth, "maybe you can speak with Father Godfred. He will know how to comfort you."

"He knows already," she whispered, "perforce, he knows."

The last three words came out as a prolonged sigh as if wrenched from the heart. A pang of jealousy shot through me.

So, Ecgwynn was able to confide in the priest and not in her brother. Such a stupid reaction lasted but a moment. Was not the cleric called by God to tend to the souls of his flock? How presumptuous on my part to suppose I might replace my sister's confessor.

A series of terrible thoughts passed through my mind. What was so grave as to fill Ecgwynn with anguish and drive her to seek out a priest? Was she with child? I hugged her tighter. Was I to be an uncle? Yet, my good sense told me that Ecgwynn would never lie with a man out of wedlock. It could not be so. What then? I needed to know. Else how could I help?

"Tell me what troubles you, Ecgwynn. A burden shared is half the load." I'd heard that said somewhere and repeated the words. She returned the hug.

"Oh, Ecgwulf, you are the best brother in the world! I promise you, I shall tell all as soon as I'm ready – later."

She pushed me away and closed the door in my face but with no hint of violence.

I cannot say that her promise made me feel better. I'd failed. My empty stomach rumbled. I headed for the kitchen to implore the cook for a fresh egg. There, I found her chatting with Lufe who shot me an enquiring glance.

"She will talk when she's ready," I said and shook my head before turning to the cook. "Get me a newly-laid egg, woman."

At that point, Lufe increased my worries.

"So, she will speak," the maid said, "The Lord be praised! When she does, help my mistress, Lord Ecgwulf, I beg you."

I glared at her for begging aid when she would not confide in me.

"Of course." My tone was curt. I cracked the egg the cook gave me on the edge of a table and gulped it down. Only then did I realise my tense state as my gorge rose. I hurried to the well and drew some ice-cold water, flinging handfuls onto my face before using the wooden cup to settle my breakfast. My body felt better, but my thoughts whirled in turmoil. One thing was for Ecgwynn to confide in me later, another was Lufe's distressed plea. What could be so amiss?

I had to wait until eventide as it turned out. First, sword-play with Osbald beckoned. At twilight, I wandered into the yard and found him ready and waiting.

"Lord," he grinned in gap-toothed greeting, tossing me a practice weapon, "why at this time?"

"Because, in battle, the light might not be good?" I hoped this was the answer because no other came to mind.

"That's it!" He leapt forward to deliver an underarm thrust. Only, it did not take me by surprise. I am a quick learner and, wary of Osbald's wiles, I swatted the blow aside with ease. The warrior knew when to praise, when to encourage and, more importantly, when to punish. In the dim light, I learnt more in an hour than I had in all my childhood engagements. The feeble light had gone so Osbald called an end to the practice but did not resist one more sly blow after he had done so. I strode back to the hall with my mind alert and refreshed, the anxieties of the morning almost forgotten.

Almost, but awaiting me, Ecgwynn greeted me with, "Ecg-wulf, why you are quite grown, nearly a man!"

"I *am* a man!"

"Men! My undoing!"

What was she saying? My disbelieving brain returned to her being with child. Thankfully, I bit off the attempt to ask her straight out and changed the question. "Are you willing to talk, sister?"

"As ready as I'll ever be," she said, her tone sour.

I clapped my hands, a servant hurried over. "Winstan, fetch me ale and two cups." I addressed Ecgwynn as he hastened away. "I have a raging thirst after sword practice."

"How goes it with Osbald?"

"When he's not imitating a charging bull, he plays the sly fox. I doubt I could find a better teacher in the whole of Kent."

"Let's hope you won't need your skills too soon," she murmured, clasping her hands together.

"The Danes have been quiet hereabouts for too long, Minster ever promises ripe pickings!"

"Oh, if I become a nun, it's there I shall go, I'd expect my protector to keep me safe." She squeezed my arm and admired its hardness.

"A nun! You are not serious. In that case, I'd never become an uncle," I led her to the subject of babes so she might confess easier if my wild thought was right.

Instead, she pursed her lips and widened her eyes. "Why be an uncle when you can be a father?" This, she accompanied with a malicious smile.

"Oh, I thought—"

"What did you think? That I am with child? For shame!"

"I-I..."

"Heed me well, I've found the right man, I would love to make you an uncle, but..."

"But?"

"It is why I weep. I wish to marry Edward, God knows I do!"

"Edward? The tall fellow you were walking out with the other day?"

"Father was worried. He knew about us – me and Edward."

"Why was he worried?"

Her eyes brimmed with tears, but I, occupied with pouring another ale, did not notice.

"Because of who he is," her voice caught.

I looked up. "Why, is he an outlaw?"

She laughed and fought back tears. "Oh, Ecgwulf, you are a

donkey! First, you have me with child, then you saddle the babe with an outlaw father! Is this what you think of your sister?" Her tone had become reproving and harsh.

"Ecgwynn, you are more precious to me than life," her lovely dark grey eyes beguiled me, "but if you talk in riddles, what am I supposed to think? Dealing with women is harder than fighting the Danes!"

"Edward is no outlaw! He's the King's son! He loves me and would have us wed."

"So, the riddle is not in your words, but in your very being! You are in love with the aetheling, he loves you and wishes to wed, yet you close yourself in your chamber to sob your heart out! I don't think I'll ever understand women!"

"You won't if you don't hear them out."

I took a deep draught of my ale, smacked my lips, and said, "Go on."

"The problem is not Edward or I, but rather the King. Alfred does not approve."

"Why ever not? You are young and pretty and from a noble family."

"Thank you, brother. But the family is the problem! King Alfred sees Edward as the future of the kingdom. Wedlock for him is a tool for a marriage alliance that cannot be wasted on a mere noblewoman from the obscure reaches of Kent. He has greater ambitions for his firstborn son...and for his kingdom." The first tear trickled down her cheek.

"What does Edward say about this?"

She rubbed a sleeve in an angry gesture across her face and sniffed, "He says he loves me and will wed me anyway."

"That's all right then."

"Of course it isn't! He cannot defy his father, the King!"

"But to be sure, if you wed in church and Edward takes you to meet him, the King will accept the deed is done."

"But will he cast out Edward and turn to his cousin Aethelwold, who has ever eyed the throne with yearning?"

"I don't know what to say."

"There is nothing you can say, dear Ecgwulf! Don't you suppose we thought of everything?"

"What does Edward mean to do?"

"He has spoken with Father Godfred who will wed me here."

I leapt to my feet and hastened around the table to embrace her.

"Ecgwynn! My sister wed with the aetheling. One day you will be the Lady of West Seaxa!"

She shrugged me off and gave me a stare that, frankly, chilled my heart.

"That's just it!" she cried, "I'll never be able to call myself that. King Alfred would never allow it! He m-might even order me slain."

I stared at her, aghast. She meant what she said. "Nobody will harm you while there's breath in—"

"Oh, Ecgwulf! Why does it have to be like this?"

"Have you consented to the wedding?"

"Father Godfred says he will not wed us unless you give me away," she said, her voice resigned.

"My consent?"

She nodded. "Father died, so it must be you, Ecgwulf."

I sat back down and reached for the ale, thinking hard. Edward wanted the wedding. King Alfred did not. Clear enough, Ecgwynn loved Edward. Would God help the lovers or would the will of His anointed King prevail? What was I to do? How to decide, especially now, tired and with my thoughts befuddled by ale?

"Let me think about this, Ecgwynn. It's all so sudden."

"Think on this too. Edward will not announce the wedding. He wants to keep it secret."

"Then I must talk with Edward before I give my consent. Will he come to Sondwic?"

She sipped at her ale for the first time. Setting the cup down with care, she smiled at me with a semblance of hope in her fair countenance, "He will come before the moon is full."

"Good night, sweet sister. Do not fret. All will be well." With my voice full of certainty, I hoped to give reassurance I did not share in my heart.

I strode out into the night and stared up at the moon. Another four days and it would be full. But would my ideas be as clear as the full moon? At that moment, I was confused. To give my consent would be to set myself against my king to whom I swore loyalty. To withhold it would break the heart of my beloved sister. What if they wed in secret and had children? Would Edward recognise them before the eyes of the world?

Oh, why did I, at my young age, have to face such hard choices? Why had Father died? What would he have done? It was too much to carry on my own shoulders. First, I must talk with Father Godfred and then face up to Edward. *Strength and wisdom* – it always came down to the same things!

3

SONDWIC, KENT, 894 AD

The last of the light was fading when Osbald called a halt to our practice. A tall figure with thick chestnut-brown hair and beard had not penetrated my consciousness, he had been studying the pair of us at our pretend warfare. That much was clear from the conversation ensuing after his call.

"Lord Ecgwulf! A word if I may!"

A head taller than me but thin as a hoe and slightly curve-shouldered, nonetheless, the fellow had a force of character conveyed by his sharp, piercing gaze. Those hazel eyes fixed me now in assessment from head to toe.

"Goodness," he said, "after that display, far rather you were a friend than a foe."

"I know not why we should be either. I just clapped eyes on you for the first time," I said, disregarding what I supposed was meant to be a compliment.

"One so young has no right to wield a weapon with such skill."

There was no ignoring praise so clearly spelt out.

I waved a vague hand toward Osbald's back as he headed

back to his home. "My tutor doubtless would disagree, for I need learn much yet. Still, I thank you for your kind words, friend."

"Friends by all means," he smiled, "but we ought to become so much more."

I pride myself on my quick wits, glancing up at the star-studded sky, at the moon beaming down with a full-blown smile, my bewilderment took me but a second to resolve. The time to thrust out a hand for him to clasp.

"You must be Edward the aetheling, son of our beloved King Alfred."

He seized my hand and hauled on it as I meant to kneel before him.

"Stay!" he said, "there is a time for everything. First, we must talk."

"Let us retire to my hall, where we can take refreshment."

Would Ecgwynn be waiting to join in the uncomfortable discussion I intended to have with her suitor? Half of me hoped not, the other, the insecure part of callow youth, still sought a figure of guidance. No sign of her, so my preoccupations were in vain.

"Winstan!" I called, and the servant came apace to my service. "Fetch our guest the best mead!" I turned to face my visitor. "Forgive me, I ought to have asked whether you preferred another tipple?"

"Mead will be fine! So, you guessed who I am. I see Ecgwynn's high esteem is well merited."

"Lord," I said, "it is mutual, which is why I cannot give my consent to such an alliance."

The colour drained from the aetheling's face, his lips tightened. He stared down a long, straight nose with its prominent arched bridge. The former friendliness quite disappeared from his countenance.

"What are you saying, Lord Ecgwulf?"

"My Prince, I cannot allow my sister's heart to be shattered."

"Then do not—"

He cut off his remark for Winstan approached with mead and glasses. With approval, I smiled at the servant who had chosen Father's best Frankish glasses. He would bring these glasses forth only for special occasions. But, Edward, used to finery, could not be expected to notice the honour. Mead poured, Winstan bowed and moved away.

"You were saying?"

"Do not break my betrothed's heart. It is in your power to grant your consent. No priest will wed us without it."

"Indeed, Lord! Forgive my impertinence, but what about your father's consent? Is that not more important?"

The piercing eyes flashed. Had I touched a nerve? I'd say so, going by the acidity of his tone.

"My father will get used to it, once we are espoused."

"Pardon me if I talk plainly, my Prince, but did you think through all the consequences?"

"Speak your mind to the full," but he failed to veil the irritation underlying the words.

"You are young and healthy, thank the Lord, so is Ecgwynn. If it is God's will, you will beget many strong babes. What is to become of them?"

I raised my glass of mead to him, more to gain time for my argument, though heaven knew I had a fierce thirst after my exertions. The aetheling matched my gesture and drank with evident satisfaction.

"Mmm, good." he murmured his appreciation before taking up the discussion once more, "What would become of them? What is your meaning?"

"Lord, if the children are the fruit of a secret wedding, in the eyes of the world they would be bastards."

Plainer than that I could not say. His eyes darkened, and, for a moment, I feared he would rise and walk away. But he had not done with me.

"Hark, Lord Ecgwulf, I love your sister. What man would not? My father is not old, but he is not in the best of health. The threat of the Danes wearies him. Were God to grant me a son, my father would achieve his dearest wish – the throne secured for two generations."

"Pardon my ignorance, Lord Edward, but our King would want your marriage to be, how can I put it..."

"More advantageous?" he thrust the words into my mouth.

"Ay. My family is loyal, as your grandsire well knew, but we command too few estates for a *meaningful* alliance."

"Ecgwulf, go hang your *meaningful alliance!* I love Ecgwynn, there's an end to it!"

"Then wed her in the full light of day for all the world to see!"

These words revealed the extent of my ingenuous youth, and the aetheling understood as much. Hence, he kept his temper in check and sought to win me by explanation.

"You know that cannot be! Within days of a proclamation from the pulpit, my father would be alerted and send warriors to stop the wedding by force of arms. The marriage must be secret, in a church, and in the sight of God. What happens afterwards, dear Ecgwulf, we shall leave to the Almighty. Do you not have faith in Him?"

"Ay, but..." the argument was slipping inexorably toward the aetheling.

His intelligence was such that he knew it and seized the moment. "I see I have won you round, friend. Thus, not only

4

THE KINGDOM OF DUBLIN, 889 AD

"Sire, dire news!" The messenger knelt before Constantin Mac Aeda, or Coìseam Mac Aoidh, the name he preferred in his native Pictish language.

"Sire, you say?" asked Constantin, incredulous at the word.

"Ay, Lord," the gruff bearer of dispatches said, "I am here to report the death of your cousin King Domnall."

"How? Where?"

"In battle, slain by the Vikings led by King Harald Fairhair at Dunnottar."

"And our people, how do they fare?"

"Grievous events, Lord, the Norsemen devastate wherever they set foot. Our folk see you as their saviour. You must sail with us at once!"

"So, the *dàsachtach* is no more," Constantin murmured, giving his cousin the '*madman*' epithet he had gained himself due to his uncontrollable, violent temper. In equal measure, he was saddened and relieved that Domnall had died.

Gathering the few belongings he cared to take with him to the Kingdom of Alba, Constantin reflected on the workings of fate. He had been orphaned at the age of eight when they killed his father, Aed. Giric took the throne. One of his first acts was to exile Constantin and his cousin Domnall overseas to live with their aunt, Màel Muir, married to the King of Dublin. A loving woman, she brought up the boys as sons but had a hard time with the *dàsachtach*. On occasion, his unruliness touched upon the insane, like when he set fire to a dozing ealdorman's beard. This jest provoked the onset of a malady to the white-bearded counsellor. Domnall refused to admit the stupidity of the prank and resented his subsequent punishment, so much so that his aunt's pet dog was later found dead in a pool of blood.

No-one could prove the *dàsachtach* was to blame, but suspicion hung over him for a long time. Maids complained bitterly that he slapped their bottoms with such force it made them drop what they were carrying. He was so crafty no-one ever caught him in the act. The first few years in his aunt's household were hard for Constantin, who learned to defend himself against his tumultuous cousin and his flailing fists.

The Kingdom of Dublin, in a state of constant war with its neighbours over territorial claims, saved Constantin from further beatings at Domnall's hands. Recognising an outlet for her ward's vicious nature, Màel Muir persuaded her husband to take the elder of the cousins with him into battle. Domnall had shown promise at weaponry practice, but Constantin believed he was the more skilful of the two.

Whenever he overcame his cousin in the courtyard under the watchful eye of their tutor, he received a beating afterwards from Domnall in private. This made him cautious and crafty in his dealings with the *dàsachtach,* as people began to call the hot-headed youth. Constantin was not too proud to let a strike slip under his guard when he could have parried it with ease. Nor did he explain his poor defence when admonished by his teacher. He considered it better to lose face than to have it pummelled by his mad cousin. Some years on and Constantin was drafted into the battles where he gained respect as a reliable warrior. Domnall acquired a different reputation, deriving from his berserk behaviour on the battlefield meaning the humblest subject called him by his well-known nickname. Domnall would trouble Constantin no more, but he left the Kingdom of Alba in a woeful state for him to remedy.

Fortune smiled on Constantin; it came in the form of settled weather for the crossing of the Irish Sea and the onset of gales once he was ashore. The heavy rain, driven by unceasing winds, set in for long, dreary weeks. Constantin's luck holding, it meant to the Vikings an end to campaigning for that season. The roads became impassable, even skilful sailors would not risk their vessels being driven on the jagged rocks that lay insidious inches below the surface of the sea or rose majestically and forbiddingly above the waves.

The crowning took place at Scone in 900. Constantin set the tone for his reign by demanding the ceremony take place in the presence of the *Breccbennach,* the holy reliquary containing relics of Saint Columba.

The seriousness with which the thirty-winters-old King Constantin II, named after his grandsire, swore to protect his people resurfaced with the return of the Vikings. This invasion came in the third year of his reign. Ui Imair led the Norsemen, the same army that defeated Domnall. A different proposition from his cousin, Constantin carried the *Breccbennach* into battle after praying and fasting and slew the Viking leader. He associated the relics with triumph in battle, attributing victory to the intercession of the saint, ridding his land of the Norsemen for the foreseeable future. Constantin swore again to keep his people safe, but he was not averse to spreading the borders of his kingdom. Everyone wanted peace, but he also wanted wealth, that could be obtained by relieving treasure from his southern neighbours. The temptation remained constant, but wisdom prevailed. The men of the south shared an enemy with him, the dreaded Norsemen. If he kept peace with them, he could always call upon them in times of need.

First, he wanted to ensure his uncontested leadership, and to do this, he needed the support of the Ionian Church. To this end, he called a meeting with Bishop Cellach in 906. The wind whistled about their ears on the Hill of Belief, a sacred site near the royal vill at Scone. There, the two men, in a ceremony made briefer by the biting wind, pledged themselves that the ordinances and disciplines of the faith, and the laws of churches and gospels, should be kept *pariter cum Scottis*. This meant in conformity to the customs of the people. Constantin, in healing the rift his cousin had created between crown and Church, showed himself to be a wily ruler as well as a worthy warrior.

His ambitions, however, went beyond keeping his own land safe for he to cast his eyes over his borders to the west and more fatefully to the south.

5

SONDWIC, KENT, 895 AD

"We should take a ship down the Temes and up the Lygan," the Aetheling Edward said. "You have a choice of ships moored here in the Stour."

I blanched at the suggestion. Cowering against my father's cloak on the roaring, ice-cold sea, comforted by his protective arm was a thing of the past. To command a long-ship over the horizon amid the salt waves tossing was another matter.

"Do I see fear in your face, Lord Ecgwulf?" Edward jibed.

Hot denial burnt in my cheeks, for I held back rash words, bitten off by a blessed residue of good sense. At least his request came in late spring with the weather set fair, I reasoned.

"There are several seaworthy vessels," I agreed when I found my voice again.

"Then we should take as many around the Thanet ness and into the Temes as you can spare crews for. Our reception in the River Lygan might be warm," he chuckled.

The next three days passed in a bustle of preparations. I decided to leave Osbald behind, charged with protecting the settlement in our absence. He could still call on a hundred men, most of them used to fighting. On the fourth morning, with the quickening tide, we cast off, our heartfelt farewells, in my case, soon forgotten in the dread I felt as the sails unfurled. The wind-ruffled feathers of terns swooping around the masthead caught my eye, and for a foolish moment, I wished to fly away with them. Instead, two fearsome adversaries awaited me, or so I persuaded myself: the sea and the Norsemen. In truth, my real opponent stood in my own shoes – the obstacle to overcome being insecurity due to lack of experience and immaturity. If anyone dared question these things to my face, I'd draw *Breath Stealer* on him.

The prows of our warships cleft through the grey-brown waters at the mouth of the estuary, and we headed into the open sea. My arrangement to save face was with one of Father's thegns. Beforehand, in private, I told him to make silent signals to me so I should appear to be in command. To my relief, the message of his gnarled, scarred hand, hidden from general view, was clear.

A swift glance at Edward, who was staring back at the outlet whence we had sailed, convinced me he had not noticed. So, with a leap on a bench at the base of the mast, my arm clinging to the latter, I called to the steersman to veer northward along the Thanet coast. My voice rang out to him in the stern with ease, and he signalled his acknowledgement. How gratifying to see the look of approval on the face of my wife-brother. This first test of my leadership mastered, I glanced back to see our six other ships veer in our wake. The voyage to the mouth of the Temes passed without incident. The harmless passage of merchant vessels, invariably hailed in greetings from our decks, broke the monotony of the ocean's heave.

The unseeing eyes of the wolf-head prow, we fitted as a

signal of our warlike intentions, pitched over the choppy approach where the river embraced the sea. The intensity of its wooden gaze scarcely matched that of Edward as we searched warily for enemy craft. But we sought in vain. Within the hour we were amid the cries and odours of the bustling port of Lundenwic.

"Father keeps talking about repairing the stone fortifications," said Edward pointing back downstream to where the ruins of Londinium stood. "The Danes stayed there four winters past."

"Regarding the Norsemen, where is the mouth of the Lygan, do you know?"

Edward shook his mane of chestnut-brown hair.

Without continuing the conversation, I strode over to my old sea-dog adviser and bent over his grey-haired head to exchange words.

Satisfied, I straightened and roared, "Man the oars!" I cupped my hands and shouted the order to the other ships from Sondwic.

In reply to Edward's quizzical look, I explained, "One of our greybeards knows it well. We cannot enter the river under sail, and it flows into the Temes another two bends to the west, upstream."

"Excellent!" Edward clapped me on the back, his eyes flashed with eagerness.

It was at that moment I wondered whether he had a plan other than to sail into the dragon's lair. I suppose I did not ask for fear he might interpret my question as a lack of faith or worse. But I must admit to being worried. Bereft of information about King Alfred's movements and plans, we headed into the Lygan, seven ships' crews to face a Norse army – like cattle to the slaughter.

In my total ignorance of events, owing to my blissful childhood disinterest, I did not know the King camped near the Danish fortress to contain the Norsemen. Neither was I aware he had overseen the building of two fortresses lower down the Lygan, so the invaders could not get their ships back out. My relief was great when Edward chose to inform me, but it might not have been so, had I known at what precise time we were to arrive.

My first taste of warfare was from a distance and one of bitter defeat. The King's army was marching on the Danish fortress, and we were in time to watch helplessly as the defenders emerged to put their assailants to flight. Nevertheless, my initiative was later to gain me the approval of Alfred. Seeing that we were too late to join in anything but a rout, I ordered my men back to the boats and thence along the river to where the Norse long-ships rocked at their moorings under the supervision of a handful of unfortunates whom we slaughtered. We cut free the most attractive of the vessels and towed them back down the river while, as a farewell, we left the rest to blaze and darken the skies with smoke. The only part Edward played in this enterprise was to hail the new fortresses Alfred had constructed.

On seeing a small fleet approaching with a black cloud billowing behind it downstream, they had taken up their bows and raised an iron chain boom across the river to prevent passage. At Edward's bellowed command, they slackened the boom which sank to the riverbed and un-nocked their arrows. We rowed back to the Temes unmolested, cheered by having snatched a minor victory from the maws of defeat. Only later, did we learn that the Norsemen, deprived of their ships, marched overland to a place called Cwatbridge on high ground overlooking the great Saefern River. There, they built a fortress and spent the winter. By taking their vessels, we had drawn the dragon's teeth, but its fiery breath remained to ravage the land.

In the Temes, Edward insisted on leaving us at Lundenwic.

"Give Ecgwynn my love and tell her I will come as soon as I can," he instructed me, "and, Ecgwulf, today you rendered great service to your King, he shall know of it. Safeguard my wife at whatever cost!"

Upon that gratuitous admonition, he took his leave. With mixed feelings, I watched him go. Wasn't his place with his spouse? Or was it with his father, the King? In my opinion, it was both. But then, what value had my simple ponderings in a world wracked by slaughter, plunder, and destruction?

We sailed into the Stour with our trophies, a return greeted by the measured gaze of appreciation in weather-beaten, lined faces on the river bank of Sondwic. These men knew full well how much grief and havoc only one of these sleek craft could carry to innocent farmsteads and churches inland, and we had seized a dozen.

My greeting from Ecgwynn was far more emotional. She clung to me like a limpet to a rock and only after my fulsome reassurances as to Edward's wellbeing did she relax.

"Join me in a glass of mead," I suggested.

That is when she delivered her own news.

"I fear I would not keep it down, Ecgwulf. My stomach refuses anything but water in the morning."

It is true I was dulled by weariness and the strain of the last few days, so my usual quick wits deserted me on this occasion.

"Are you unwell, sister?"

Her beautiful face lit up, a teasing laugh revealed the depths of her joy and the secret her womb held, to my re-awakening acuity.

"You are with child!" I cried as if emerging from a dream, "I am to be an uncle! Winstan, where are you? You dullard! Fetch me mead!" I gazed at Ecgwynn and thought her the comeliest woman in Kent. My heart swelled. "We must celebrate," I cried, snatching up my glass and quaffing the honeyed beverage in one avid draught. "Another!" I commanded Winstan, "this is a great occasion! Shame Edward isn't here to share the moment," I said thoughtlessly and had to squeeze Ecgwynn's hand to set matters aright. I delivered his message that he would return as soon as he could and this restored Ecgwynn's smile.

"I can't wait to see his face when he hears the news!" I grinned in her face, and she nodded, not without anxiety.

"Do you think he will share our joy?"

The question struck me as ridiculous.

"Of course, he will! Why wouldn't he? I swear I know him better than you, sister."

At this, she bared her teeth and snapped, "I doubt that very much!"

"How then can you question your husband's reaction? I'm sure you will make him the happiest man in the kingdom."

"I hope his father feels the same way," she said, and her eyes gleamed with tearful brightness.

Then I remembered Edward's parting words. But first, I said, "I slew four Danes myself," and the memory of killing a man for the first time clouded my face. "We took twelve of their ships and burnt the rest of their fleet." I stared at my sister. "Edward promised me the King would know of my service. It can only help our family!"

At this, she smiled. "Father, gazing from heaven above, will be proud of you. You will become a great warrior like him."

That, of course, was my ardent desire, but first I would have to hold my place in the terrifying shield wall. What I had seen of the Norsemen's wrath made it a frightening prospect.

"Do not weep, Ecgwynn! Not on this most joyous of days. All will be well, trust me!"

Although I spoke so full of confidence, my heart was less secure. I had been confident that Alfred would thrash the Danes, the opposite had happened – so much for my certainties.

6

SONDWIC, WINTER 897 AD

The year ended hard. Disease wiped out cattle but also men and women. Neither did it spare the high and mighty. So desperate was the plight of the common folk that the Danes, we learnt from what news got through to us, were reported to have moved away to Northanhymbre. The more penniless of these, indeed, took their ships across the sea to the Seine.

Sondwic suffered from disease too, but not all the events were devastating. Ecgwynn gave birth to a lusty, squalling babe – a boy she named Athelstan. I chose a messenger for his closed nature and impressed upon him none other than the aetheling should learn of the birth. Days later, Edward arrived bearing gifts for his wife and son, proud and happy as a new father should be. But the presents were not all he bore. He brought a message to me from King Alfred.

"Ecgwulf, you are to return to Wintan-caestre with me. The King...my father...commands your presence."

"Did he say why, Edward?"

"He confides little in me, but he must have remembered

your name from my account of the burning of the Danish fleet. When he learnt of my visit to Kent, he issued the order."

"But he does not know about Athelstan?"

"Perish the thought! Good Lord, no!"

Better not to react to this provocation and keep my thoughts to myself. What did Alfred want of me? His summons could not have been worse timed in my opinion. There was much to do in our settlement. The command to leave drove home my deep fondness for Sondwic. The town held no secrets for me, knowing as I did, every nook and cranny in the place. Being Ealdorman meant I occupied myself with the daily problems of the townsfolk, just as my father used to do. So, I spent the days before Edward wrenched himself away from his family organising late-winter tasks. These included caulking the boats, repairs to the riverside structures and defences, and the rota for the Dane-watch patrols. The farmers, governed by the weather, could be left to their own devices.

As soon as a settled spell set in, Edward decided to depart, to my renewed disapproval choosing to separate from his wife and child. I persuaded a returning trader – a tin merchant – to give us passage as far as the port of Hamwic. The place was new to me, but what Edward assured me once was a royal vill and a thriving emporium with the minting of its own silver coins, appeared mournful and run down. This, he said with a bitter tone, was the result of repeated Viking raids. Many craftsmen and businesses were forced to shelter behind the walled safety of nearby Wintan-caestre.

The contrast between the two towns shocked me. The royal burh of Wintan-caestre offered everything a man might need, including shops with exotic spices, tin, copper, and bronze ware. The bustling coming and going made it hard to find anyone not occupied with a productive activity. The exceptions were the street entertainers, tumblers, jugglers and tricksters, the beggars and the painted whores, all of whom vied for our attention as we hurried past. The fresh sea air I breathed daily in Sondwic became a distant memory. Here, the temptation was not to breathe at all, so foul were the odours.

At the carved doorway of the royal palace, guards in full armour relieved us of our weapons. I hated being separated from *Breath Stealer,* but blades were not permitted inside the king's mead hall. Inside, the air was sweet with the scent of the strewn lavender we crushed underfoot. The sumptuousness of the surroundings was beyond even my flights of fancy. The bright colours of the wall pilasters depicted strange biting beasts. Intricate woven tapestries hung between them, and these, along with the soaring cross tie-beams, bespoke the importance of the King of West Seax.

In the daytime, the hall was not as crowded as at feasting, but the servants, guards, and the King's advisers still created a hubbub of voices and movement. King Alfred, leaning over a small table, sat on a throne whence he pored over a chessboard, although I saw no opponent.

"He often plays alone," Edward explained, drawing me towards the King. "He says no-one gives him a good enough game. I swear I can beat him if he only allows me the chance."

We halted before the throne.

The King did not look well. His face was drawn and pale, enhancing the black rings darkening the slack skin beneath his eyes. Grey hair at the temples pushed from under the gold ringlet he wore, instead of a heavy ceremonial crown, to denote his kingship. Edward cleared his throat to break the King's concentration and make him aware of our presence.

"Ah, Edward, my son! Did you journey well?"

"By sea, father, as far as Hamwic."

"Ah, by sea...ay..." the king seemed distracted. Were his thoughts still on the chess? I soon found they were not. "Who is your companion?" The sharp eyes, so similar to Edward's, turned to me.

I affected a bow and waited.

"This is Ealdorman Ecgwulf of Sondwic, Father. He who–"

"Burnt the Viking fleet," Alfred finished, but his smile was puzzled. "So young? I expected you older, Ealdorman."

"Ecgwulf wields a fine blade," Edward interjected.

"You came by sea," Alfred took up his earlier thought. "That is good." He stood, or rather, sprang to his feet and clapped his hands. A servant hurried over. "Fetch my blue cloak, fellow," he commanded and to us confided, "We must take a boat to the coast."

"But we've just come from the coast, Father," Edward failed to keep the irritation from his voice.

"And now you are going back there." Alfred's tone brooked no gainsaying.

The King might not have boasted a healthy countenance, but the vigour of his stride past the cathedral to a quay on the River Aire suggested reserves of strength. Once in the barge, manned by six oarsmen, the King struck up conversation with me. The workmanship of my sword hilt caught his eye, so he asked to see *Breath Stealer*. "Made in Frankia, I'll wager."

"Indeed, Sire. My father wielded it before me in the service of King Aethelred."

"My beloved father."

"Ay, lord."

"And will you wield it for me, Ecgwulf?"

"At your command."

The King smiled and handed back the weapon, pommel first. "Splendid! I fear it will be the case sooner rather than later."

My heartbeat quickened. What was the King implying?

"It has been a hard winter, Ealdorman. The pestilence has taken many beasts, but worse, far worse, many of my thegns. The Bishop of Hrofescaester has departed this life, God rest his soul. Your part of the world, isn't it? And another, Coelmund, a trusted ealdorman in Kent; Bertulf ealdorman in Est Seax; Wulfred ealdorman in Hamtunscir; Elhard Bishop of Dorchester; Eadul, my thegn in Suth Seax," he sighed. "And it did not spare those nearer my palace, Bernuff governor of Wintan-caestre, and, not least, Egulf my horse-thegn." His voice tailed away full of sorrow.

"I am sorry, Sire."

"Do not be," the piercing hazel eyes bored into mine. "I forgot to hand you the deeds, back in Wintan-caestre."

What did he mean? I frowned, puzzled, but decided to hold my tongue.

"Deeds?" Edward's curiosity got the better of him.

"Ay, deeds. So that our young Ealdorman may own the lands commensurate with his new position."

"Position?" the aetheling pressed.

"Blast you, Edward! Must you repeat my every word?" The king stared at me. "Forgive my son," Alfred said, "now what was I saying? Ah, as a token of my gratitude for your service on the Lygan – otherwise one of my few failures – I decided to give you all of Ealdorman Coelmund's estates. I am sure you can manage them well enough from Sondwic. Coelmund died of the accursed ague along with his brother and nephew, hence there are no heirs to the lands. So, you need but present yourself...in due course...*in due course*."

I pondered on the stress the king placed on the repeated words but not too deeply to prevent me expressing my gratitude.

Alfred brushed my thanks aside with, "The kingdom needs stout warriors such as yourself, Ealdorman. Had it not been for your quick-thinking, we should not have rid ourselves of the Vikings after my ill-judged attack on their fortress. They wintered by the Saefern but dispersed, as you may know, to Northanhymbre and Est Anglia. They will sail forth from there in their esks to harass our lands as soon as the spring settles into summer, Ecgwulf. But you will be ready for them."

"*I*, Lord?"

"You are to be commander of my fleet. That is why we are heading to the coast so you may see your ships and make all the necessary arrangements. While the cattle and my people were stricken by illness, I have not been idle. All winter, when the weather allowed, my shipwrights have laboured on the task. The Vikings will meet their match under your guidance. If I am right...and when am I not? They will come, you will destroy them. Lord Ecgwulf, I designed the vessels myself so they might be most serviceable, but hold! I shall say no more until you feast your eyes upon them. The longer the Norsemen delay, the more time we will have to add to their number, but I can promise you eight are ready." He lapsed into silence.

Edward nudged me and smiled encouragement.

"It is an honour you bestow on me, Sire," I said, but the King was distracted, watching a water vole plunge into the river. The current, slower here, where the watercourse was broader, still aided the oarsmen to make swift progress. How far had we come? The unmistakeable salty smell of the sea in the air and the mewing of the wheeling gulls meant we were nearing the end of the four-league trip.

Our river came to a confluence with another, and, offshore, a sight only a delirious fever might have suggested to my brain met my eyes. Riding at anchor in the bay were eight magnificent, huge ships. They were unlike anything I had seen before, not shaped either after the Frisian or the Danish type and twice as long.

King Alfred could not contain his eager scrutiny of my face any longer. "Five of them have eighty oars, and three have sixty! They are higher than the enemy's esks and, I trust, steadier and swifter. Pull alongside!" he ordered the steersman.

Ingenious, I thought. The Vikings, with their superior vessels and seamanship, ever destroyed the craft we sailed to counter them with. The King's brilliant mind was now turning the situation in our favour. We clambered aboard, and for the first time, I walked the decks of what was to become *my* ship. I would have the name *Breath Stealer* carved into her prow so my sword and my ship should be as one.

The King commanded me to stay and finish all the arrangements for manning and making the ships ready for war. To my surprise, he embraced me and whispered, "Lord Ecgwulf, destroy the Vikings and leave not a trace!" A leg over the gunwale, he bade me farewell before scrambling back into his barge. I turned to Edward whose duty was to follow him. "Will you tell him about little Athelstan?"

"There is a season for every purpose," he quoted a familiar biblical passage.

I thought it better to stay silent and, with mixed feelings, watched him swing down to the waiting boat. My opinion of Edward was also conflicting. I found it hard to warm to him, but it was clear that his words to the King on my behalf must have been glowing. Thanks to his intercession, at the tender age of eighteen winters, I stood in command of a fleet and was the master of extensive lands in Kent. Above all, although it was still a secret, I was wife-brother to the heir to the throne of West Seax, likeable or not. The reality of responsibility struck me. When would I see my beloved home in Sondwic again? My new work beckoned and overruled my thoughts.

Enough of this useless rumination.

Standing alone on the deck of an empty ship, I jolted out of my complacency. I had no desire to dive into the ice-cold sea and swim in search of other life. I scanned the shore and noticed a hut. My cold hands cupped around my mouth, I hailed anyone who might hear. But there was no movement. The daylight was dwindling. I guessed another hour would bring darkness. My plight was dire without heat and exposed to the biting wind sweeping off the ocean. I cried out again and again to no avail; only the answering call of seabirds broke the silence. There was no question of moving the craft on my own. Desperate for a solution, I prowled the deck but found that the shipbuilders had left it clear. There was not so much as a rag out of place, let alone anything to use as a blanket. Only with nightfall did I resign myself to my fate. It was too early to sleep, so I curled up under the shelter of the windward gunwale, pulled my cloak tight around my trembling body, and settled down to think.

The complete absence of labourers puzzled me. Was the hut for storage? Why had Alfred not thought about the predicament he was leaving me in? But that was unfair – for it had not occurred to me when he left.

Hapless, I stared at the magnificent display of the stars above the gentle sway of the mast. Strange how the sight of the heavens reminds us of our insignificance. Earlier, I considered myself...goodness knows, how important in my new role. Teeth chattering uncontrollably, I risked death by exposure to the chill probing of the wind. As inconsequential and vulnerable as a swallow failed to fly to warmer climes. At that moment, my life was so unimportant that no-one would be present at my demise. I tugged the cloak over my head for protection but only succeeded in suffocating my breathing and uncovering my thighs to the cold. Gulping in air, I restored the garment to its former position and prayed for survival.

Prayer was never my strong point, and I abandoned my

efforts in favour of considering the commitment the king had entrusted to me. Assuming I survived the night, the next day, I'd need to set foot ashore and make arrangements to gather a crew for each of the eight ships. How that could be done was a mystery. That the vessels were superb was unquestionable, but they would not sail themselves, and had the king not spoken about building more while awaiting the return of the Vikings? Anxiety gripped me. "What if they come on the morrow?" I murmured to the Dog Star, one I could locate without difficulty. "We shall not be ready!"

Sleep, an unexpected blessing, I believed impossible in my wretchedness, perhaps brought on by the rhythmic rocking of the ship, enfolded me. Daylight, accompanied by the cacophony of seabird cries, woke me. Numb with cold, head spinning from a lack of food and drink, I hauled myself upright, stamping on the deck to restore life to my chilled bones. My prayer was answered, I was alive, but I knew another night like that would be the end of me. Before buckling *Breath Stealer* around my waist, I decided to run from the prow to the stern of the ship, leaping over any obstacles in my way. A casual onlooker would have thought a madman had taken possession of the vessel. But what did I care? The numbness passed at once; and warmed and breathless from my exertions, head spinning, I stared toward the land and considered whether to swim the hundred and fifty yards to shore. I am not a strong swimmer, and the thought of plunging into the icy water repelled me. It was out of the question, but another night on board...? What was I to do?

The uncertainty lasted for an hour after dawn when, praise the Lord, a fisherman in a small boat pulled out from the river and rowed into the bay. In a matter of moments, my wild arm-waving and shouting alerted him to make him change direction and bump his little, blessed craft against the hull of the warship. Never was a man so welcome to my sight!

While he rowed to set his nets, I tried to discover the local knowledge I needed. But the fellow, overawed by having a lord in his boat or maybe too simple to understand my questions, was of little help. I gathered there was a small settlement up the river whence he had emerged, but whether it was the river or the village named Test, I could not ascertain. He nodded with a rotten-toothed grin when I asked to be taken to his village. There, for sure, I would find someone with whom I could hold a meaningful conversation.

So it proved. Although I did not find anyone who had worked on the shipbuilding, the local lord was well-informed. The chief shipbuilder, a certain Randal, had returned to his family in Hamwic to await the arrival of the King's man. That hitherto unidentified person now beamed at the lord and presented himself. After pleasantries, he, by now aware of the awful night I had spent, called for food and drink. Along with this, my spirits were restored by his directions for finding Master Randal. The task would prove easy because his house stood between the small St Mary's Church and a smithy. Indeed, the kindness of my host extended to the offer to accompany me on horseback to this destination.

By noon, I was sitting by Master Randal's hearth, supping the ale his wife offered. The overnight ordeal faded into nothingness when he produced a bag of coins entrusted to him by Alfred and to be consigned to me. They were to be used to muster and pay for crew and for the building of other ships. The King's trust with his money was not absolute, as I found when Randal handed me a sealed letter. Upon opening it, I discovered the exact amount the bag ought to contain written in the King's hand. I decided to count it later, so as not to get our relationship off to a bad start. Instead, I talked over my plan to gather all the crew from the town of Hamwic and Randal agreed.

"Since the last Viking raid, Lord, many sailors are unable to find work." He also proved invaluable in suggesting a rate of pay that would bring the men without it being overgenerous.

I found an inn which I could use as a base. There, I discovered that Randal was an honest man because the contents of the bag, gold and silver coins, tallied exactly with the King's written total. Had he been a rogue, with that amount, he could have fled overseas and led the life of a lord. At this thought, I promised myself I would make the shipwright a rich man if it were within my possibilities.

The business of raising almost six hundred men turned out to be easier than I'd hoped. The down payment of five scillingas a man proved an irresistible lure along with the promise of a retainer to be paid every full moon. To add to these were the Frisian warriors the King had promised me. The Frisians were among several other races who received a warm welcome at King Alfred's court. They had a seething hatred of the Norsemen and were renowned fighters and would be a fine addition to my force.

A visit to the blacksmith and an order placed for four hundred spearheads and the same number of axe-heads transformed him into the happiest man in Hamwic. He explained how he would have to engage other smiths to help him. I did not care a whit so long as the order was met as soon as possible and at the right price. There remained only to organise a team of lookouts along the coast charged with the task of giving early warning of Viking presence. Four men, I reckoned enough for this, but it meant the purchase of four horses. King Alfred must have calculated the cost of all this because the money provided more than covered my expenditure.

I sauntered through the regularly laid-out lanes of the town, wrinkling my nose at the stench and once more longing for the fresh air of Sondwic. When would I see home and family again? Strange to tell, the thought spurred me on with the task at hand, perhaps a desire to get it over. It meant I found my way to Randal again, where I brought up the last two matters to resolve.

"The King ordered the building of other ships before the Vikings return."

"That's all well and good, Lord Ecgwulf, but if the Norsemen are coming, they will come before the summer is out. Not even they relish our seas in the autumn fogs and winter gales. Do you know how long it takes to build one of those beauties?"

I shrugged and shook my head.

"With a full workforce, I'd say it can't be done in less than two months, and that's working all day, every day except Sunday."

An idea struck me. "We can use the extra sailors I hired as a workforce to lift and carry for your skilled men."

This pleased Randal, who agreed it would expedite matters. Of course, it did, to the extent that we had one more ship to add to our fleet when the news broke of six Viking ships sighted off the Isle of Wight.

7

SOUTH COAST OF ENGLAND, 897 AD

The time it took to organise the men and ships ready for combat, sad to relate, enabled the Norsemen to raid Defnascir. They did much mischief there and everywhere on the seacoast. Our nine vessels, sailing in line, cut a splendid figure as we bore out into the open sea with one objective in mind – to spring a trap. If we bottled the Vikings in a cove or the mouth of an estuary, we would be sure to prevail with our superior might.

That was exactly how we found them. Not knowing the land thereabouts, to this day, I know not which inlet it was. Thence three craft hove in sight with the intimidating images of their sails – a black, wide-winged raven, a grey wolf's head and one simple design of broad, red and white stripes. A sharp-eyed lookout pointed out another three ships beached in the estuary. But grounded, they had to wait for the tide turning. The steersman reacted to my order, and we directed our fearsome prow to intercept the three vessels. As we drew near, the Norsemen pulled in their oars and unhooked round shields from the gunwales. Seizing a chain with a grapple attached, I swung it underarm, and a pair of men I had positioned along the side for the same purpose copied my action. The three hooked irons soared on board the esk and bit into the inside of the wooden gunwale. My men hauled on the chains, and although the enemy hacked at them with axes and pounded them with hammers, they did not succeed in freeing them. The shudder as the hulls clashed nigh knocked me off balance.

The difference between the vessels now was plain to see. Our craft was longer and higher in the water. The Norsemen could not board upwards, but we leapt down on them.

"Spears!" I yelled.

My single-word command was sufficient for a hail of iron-tipped shafts to fall on the enemy. This created the disarray I sought because the heavy ash poles impaled in their wooden shields rendering them useless.

"Board!"

We outnumbered them three to one, so the slaughter of Danes was frightful to behold, and yet, the fierce Viking warriors sold their lives at great cost. I accounted for several but had to use every trick Osbald had taught me to survive the ferocious resistance. Their stalwart defiance was the undoing of the King's reeve, Lucomon, fighting to my left and of a Frieslander named Wulfheard to my right. When not one of the fiends remained alive, I ordered oil thrown over the bodies and hacked the grapples free before I thrust a fiery torch into the vessel. Clambering aboard the *Breath Stealer*, a rapid glance told me that war raged in another esk pinned by one of our vessels but that the third was fleeing followed by seven of our ships. My main concern was that the blazing ship, now a hellish sight as the sail caught and sent a pillar of flame skyward, should not drift towards us. My urgent shouted commands caused our steersman to turn us to catch the wind and fill our sail to speed us away from the floating pyre.

Our seven ships, far swifter than the esk, drew level, and we grappled the prey. Now, I was certain that soon the third would meet the fate of the others. Looking astern, I saw our remaining ship pull free, and in its wake, the first smoke billow from the wallowing esk. Satisfied, we held our course to join the other vessels to lay by to view the spectacle of destruction on the last enemy craft. The harsh cheers of our men from all six onlooking ships must have heartened the attackers, in the same way as the two billowing columns of smoke behind us weakened Viking resolve. Whatever the truth of the matter, in a short time, this ship too remained without a living pirate.

Once the bodies and vessel burnt, I shouted another series of commands, first, to my steersman and to the others of our fleet to follow me. We escaped the flying sparks and greedy flames of the esk and returned to the estuary where the ebbing tide commenced its flow. The wait for the tide had prevented the Norsemen from fleeing with their booty and their lives.

We stood off, and patience repaid us when the raiders floated free of the beach and rowed out to meet us. I stared in wonderment at the courage of the hapless foe. In the face of such odds to make straight for battle and not to flee filled me with admiration. But hatred of Danes was in my blood, and the thought of what they had wreaked inland, not to mention our losses, meant I had no merciful thoughts to spare on them.

Setting aside personal glory for the benefit of my weak-ened crew, I shouted to those ships that had not yet fought to engage with the enemy. They were fresh and eager for battle. The outcome, given this and our superiority, thanks to King Alfred's cunning, I took for granted. To my satisfaction, two more Danish esks burnt and sank as funeral pyres. What happened with the third? It wrecked. But I would not know why till back at anchor. Its crew managed to break free of the grapples but hampered by losses, rowing against the current sweeping them onto the rocky coast of Suth Seax proved impossible. Struggling ashore from the wreck, the survivors ran into King Alfred's men, who were watching the battle from dry land. Captured and taken to the King in Wintan-caestre, he, to the joy of the resentful populace, ordered them to be hanged.

The news of our victory spread throughout the kingdom and beyond. Our valiant foes made us pay a heavy toll for this success. The Vikings dispatched sixty-two of our men, but their dead totalled one hundred and twenty, and none of the raiders who had sailed into the Solent survived. The welcome period of peace saw our shipyard on the Aire established, whose mouth was an ideal launching site while the nearby forests of Hamtunscir yielded no shortage of wood. The West Seax were, at last, ready to face the Norsemen at sea.

The autumn brought mixed weather, and by the month of October, it became too unsettled to risk our men and ships. Once safely harboured, I was free to return to Kent. There, I intended to survey my new estates before returning to Sondwic.

Before I travelled to Kent, I had to gain permission from the King, who received me with warmth. In truth, the triumph was more his thanks to the provision of such magnificent vessels, and I was not hesitant in telling him so.

"Of course, you must go to your lands in Kent, Ealdorman." Alfred smiled. "I shall oversee the building of more ships. We know full well that the Viking scourge is far from ended. They are sure to react to this defeat. That is why I expect you to come back to Wintan-caestre in the spring."

"It shall be so, Sire."

I left with his blessing but, before leaving, sought out the aetheling. Edward decided to accompany me, and, to justify his departure, he told his father he intended to strengthen the defences of Lundenwic. This was something he held dear and, so, a partial truth.

The delay at Wintan-caestre and our overland journey gave time for news of the Viking defeat to travel ahead of us from village to village and pulpit to pulpit. As is the case with word of mouth information, the farther afield it travels, the more it becomes magnified.

When my road and that of Edward parted, I received a hero's welcome on my new estates. People left their toil to line the streets to cheer the new lord in the villages. I do not think I misheard when one father pointed me out to his small son with the words *Ecgwulf the Dane-slayer!* It would be a falsehood if I said that this did not make me swell with pride. Priests condemn vainglory as a sin, but the merciless fury of the Danes meant our folk revelled in their undoing, and I was happy to vaunt my part in it.

My inspection of the land and the accounts over, I left for Sondwic contented for the competent running of the estates by the steward and reeve. These lands together with my father's made me a wealthy man. Life seemed perfect on that crisp autumn day. Little did I know it was about to get better before it worsened.

Better, because when I arrived home, Ecgwynn greeted me with my two-month-old niece, Aethelgyth, suckling at her breast. True, I had been away a year and so missed her carrying her second child. This new addition prompted earlier misgivings about the secrecy of the marriage, and these were to be confirmed when events took a turn for the worse.

In Sondwic but two nights, on the third, I drifted into sleep only to be awakened by shouting and screaming from the opposite side of the hall. The unmistakable clash of steel warned my dull brain of fighting. A Danish raid! I admit it was my first thought. Seizing *Breath Stealer*, I dashed out of my room to see a bar of flickering light cast across the rush-strewn floor. The smiting of blades rang in my ears but also the cries for help – Edward and Ecgwynn's frantic voices. Barefoot and in breeches and shirt, heedless of my need for armour, I rushed into the bedchamber of my sister.

One glance sufficed to reveal Edward assailed by three men, fighting a desperate battle against the odds. What saved him, I think, was lack of space, so that all three could not attack at once. I shall never forget the look of grateful deliverance in Ecgwynn's face when she saw me arrive. She was cowering in a corner of the room, Aethelgyth folded in her arms and Athelstan clinging to her leg, sobbing into her nightdress.

With a cry, I leapt forward, surprise on my side. My well-honed blade sliced through the leather jerkin covering the back of the nearest intruder, who fell dying at my feet. Another spun round, so Edward faced a fair fight. Immodestly speaking, I did not. I have yet to find an opponent capable of withstanding my skills with a sword. In the time it took me to register that my adversary was not a Dane but a Saxon, he crumpled mortally wounded. Driven by battle rage, I struck Edward's assailant a mighty blow from behind and, as he teetered off-balance, my wife-brother dispatched him.

Breathless, we leaned on our swords. Edward spoke first, "Brother, you came with no time to spare!"

"I thought they were Danes. But I see I was wrong."

His next words rocked me to the core of my being.

"This is my father's doing. He sent these men."

"What are you saying?"

"Who else would want my family dead?"

"It cannot be. He would not risk the death of his son."

My words drove home. The aetheling frowned and looked puzzled.

"Who then?"

"These, we cannot ask." I nodded towards the three corpses. "Help me drag them out. This is no sight for little children.

In the morning, the would-be murderers were thrown into a pit dug in the soft un-consecrated ground near the Stour. In the vain hope of finding something that might reveal their identity, I searched their clothing, tossing the few coins found in their garments to an overjoyed by-standing beggar.

Unlike Edward, I had slept soundly. Swaying with weariness, he stood muttering about the close escape. When I tried to comfort him, he replied, "Whichever way I look at it, I come back to thinking this must have been father's doing. He wants rid of my family. Ecgwulf, we must go to Wintan-caestre to confront him."

"We?"

"I need you as a witness. My father loves you well."

I called for Osbald and charged him with organising protection day and night for Ecgwynn and the children.

I swore under my breath. When everything appeared to be so much in my favour – now I must face divided loyalties!

8

WINTAN-CAESTRE, WINTER 897 AD

The raised voice of Edward reached me through the door of the King's bedchamber. His cries alternated with periods of silence.

Inside, an acrimonious discussion was taking place. Both men were red in the face: Alfred because he had taken to his bed with a fever; Edward because he was furious.

"Are you telling me you stole away like a thief in the night to wed in secret? And you have two children? What an irresponsible fool you are, Edward!" The last words, a whisper, came uttered with great weariness.

"Athelstan is a strong little fellow. But how could you dispatch men to murder your own grandson? What kind of monster are you?"

The King's febrile eyes flashed.

"Is that what you think of me? Your own father? How could I send men if I didn't know of the child's existence? Edward, you should seek out the person responsible, who is, for sure, here in Wintan-caestre. Protect my grandson at all costs. Now leave me. We shall talk again about your misdeeds and what you must do to remedy the matter. I am tired and must rest. Tell Ecgwulf to await my call for I will see him soon."

King Alfred closed his eyes and, at once, dozed off. His health, he knew, was declining and he hoped to pass the kingdom into judicious hands, not to those of an impulsive love-struck imbecile.

I passed the time in restless pacing outside the royal bedchamber. Worry consumed me. From the start, my sister's relationship with Edward the aetheling troubled me. Neither of them understood the nature of their situation with the necessary clarity of thought I possessed. Maybe my prayers for strength and wisdom had been answered, after all. I would need both, I mused, for my meeting with King Alfred. At last, the summons came.

"Lord Ecgwulf," the King held out a bejewelled hand to be raised and kissed, "we meet sooner than expected and in a manner that grieves me."

"Sire, my advice has been ignored."

"More's the pity, Edward is an idiot! The first duty of an aetheling is to his people not to his own gratification. This situation must be resolved, Ealdorman."

I knelt by the side of the bed to better hear the feeble voice and out of deference to the man I so admired.

"The most urgent task I give you is to take your sister and my grandchildren to the court of my daughter, Aethelflaed, in Mierce. There, you will watch over them and keep them safe. Mierce is in danger. A part of it is under Danish control. Athelstan will also increase the royal presence of West Seax in the Miercian court. Without the heartland of Mierce, my dream of a united Saxon Angle-land will not be realised. You will be my trusted sword there at the service of Mierce."

"But the fleet, sire?"

Alfred sighed, "We shall find another to take your place,

my friend. As we must! Hark! Those who made an attempt on Athelstan's life will try again. Your duty as uncle is to ensure they do not succeed."

The king lay back, the greyness of his complexion made him look older and suggested to me a man with a precarious grip on life.

My own plans and dreams lay in disarray. Mierce was an alien land to me. Where Aethelflaed's palace was, I did not know. I pursed my lips, bowed, muttered obedience, and backed out of the chamber. I did not see Alfred again before my departure but received a wonderful surprise from the King. He sent gifts for Athelstan. This gesture I much appreciated for its significance. From the boy's grandfather, they marked him out as throne worthy. They included a scarlet cloak, a belt set with precious stones, and a seax with a gilded scabbard. My charge was to look after them until Athelstan was old enough to use them.

I met Edward before my departure. His aspect also troubled me since the strain of the last few days had left his noble countenance drawn and pale, a pallor enhanced by his wavy chestnut hair and beard. After scrutinising my face for I know not what sign, his eyes bored into mine.

"What did my father say to you, Ecgwulf?"

"You ought to know he ordered me to take your wife and children to your sister's court in Mierce."

"To Aethelflaed in Tame Weorth? The old fox! It solves the problem neatly."

"How so?"

His withering look stung my pride. After all, this situation was of his creation.

Edward spoke as if to a slow child.

"By sending Athelstan to Mierce, my father keeps him out

of the sight of the powerful West Seax nobles and, at the same time, asserts West Seax hegemony over that kingdom."

"Will you accompany us to Mierce?"

"I shall miss you all, Ecgwulf. How can I leave here with father's health failing? If he dies, I must be in Wintan-caestre to claim *my* throne."

"Of course."

We parted on good terms. I breathed a sigh of relief, having believed I would be forced to lose the friendship of either the King or the aetheling. As it happened, I did not have to choose. But I had to obey King Alfred and go against my will to Mierce. Kent was my homeland, and I knew little else other than the sea. How long my enforced exile would last depended on the failing strength of the King. Of course, I wished for him to live for many more years, but what I saw of him in these days made it a forlorn hope.

I reached Sondwic in time to spend Christ's Mass at home, never letting down my guard night and day over Edward's – and my – family. The winter weather made travelling with the babes impracticable. Cartwheels would churn the wet mud and sink to a standstill. Ecgwynn proved to be as dismayed as me about the command to leave our home. With the fright of the recent night-time intrusion still fresh in her mind, however, her nervousness made her consent to the move.

Easter came and went before the earth dried enough for us to depart with a canvas-covered cart furnished with beds. We delayed setting off until I completed arrangements for the running of my estates in Kent. On discovering that Tame Weorth was more than two hundred miles from Sondwic, I took a score of armed men. They would be sufficient to ward off any attack on our way. Most at risk of an outlaw ambush were the forested stretches of our journey. But I relied on the sight of armoured cavalry bearing javelins to deter all but a Danish war band. Luckily, our route would make an encounter with them improbable.

Limited by the pace of the ox-cart, it took us nigh on a whole month to reach our destination. I bore a sealed document from King Alfred to deliver to Lady Aethelflaed. Imagine my disappointment when we arrived travel-weary, at last, at the splendid hall in Tame Weorth only to discover that she had long ago travelled to Wintan-caestre. Daughterly duty urged her to be at the King's bedside since his health deteriorated alarmingly. Ealdorman Aethelred, Aethelflaed's husband, welcomed us in her stead. It was to him I consigned the missive. The document explained who we were and what was our purpose at the Miercian court.

"My Lord Ecgwulf – so you are the famous *Dane-slayer!* Your sword will be useful here in Mierce," he began, looking me over from head to toe. "Lady Ecgwynn, welcome to my hall. Your beauty cannot fail to grace it. Where are the children?"

I went to fetch Athelstan and his sister. The boy toddled beside me, and I carried the babe in my arms.

"So, these are the grandchildren of King Alfred," he sighed. "My daughter Aelfwynn is too young to wed, so this is a blessing I cannot yet enjoy." He addressed Ecgwynn with a gentle smile. "My Lady, you and your children will be safe here."

They were safe. I was not. This summer, characterised by Danish incursions into Mierce, kept Lord Aethelred involved in the constant action of repelling them. I lost count of the number of smouldering farmsteads and corpses their trails of devastation left. Hard to say what was more bitter, the acrid stench of charred timber or the bile in my mouth at the sight of slaughtered ceorls. The reputation of *Breath Stealer* preceded it to Tame Weorth, hence the lord of Mierce would not renounce its presence among his outriders.

My first action came not far from Weorgoran-caestre where the new fortress constructed by Aethelred to protect against these raiders produced the opposite effect. In my opinion, it attracted them to raid nearby out of disrespect. Alerted by the column of smoke billowing above the treetops, I halted my band of fifteen mounted warriors. I insisted on bringing Osbald with me, and to him, I turned for consultation.

"The smoke yonder is not enough for the raiders to have finished their vile work, what say you?"

Osbald stared into space, reflecting before grinning. "If we ride hard, we shall catch them at their devilry."

The dense cloud pouring from a blazing barn was more intense when we arrived. Hard-gained wheat sparkled golden in the sunlight heaped on a cart set aside by the Danes to be hauled away to satisfy their rapacious appetites. But if I had ought to do with it, they would devastate and devour no more. The folk of the homestead were putting up a stout defence from behind the palisade of the main building. A cheer and waving arms alerted the score of Vikings to our arrival, and they spun to face our galloping onslaught. It earned them arrows in the back from the defenders, and more cheers erupted as they fell. Soon we rode in among them after launching a volley of javelins, most of which met with the inevitable parrying by their gaudy shields. The Norsemen, on foot, tried to defend themselves by attacking our horses, but the well-trained war steeds were intelligent beasts. It was the devil's own job for me to remain in the saddle as my mount reared. The enraged animal crashed an iron-shod hoof down on the shoulder of a Viking who had attempted to impale his sword into its chest. Instead, *Breath Stealer* impaled *his*.

Another Dane received a pitchfork between the shoulder blades from one of the defenders whose bravery brought him out from behind the sturdy wooden gates.

Our advantage was great so that, soon, all but a few of the Danes lay dead.

"Cease!" I bellowed. "I want these alive."

It was easier said than effected. For the Danes, death in combat meant a passage to Waelheal and a seat at Odin's table. My order produced a redoubling of their efforts because my men ceased to attack on my command and limited themselves to defence. I dismounted.

"This one is mine!"

The Viking grinned and rushed at me as I hoped. His predictable assault was his undoing. To a rousing cheer, his sword went arcing into the air and my shield crashed into his jaw, sending him sprawling senseless to the ground. My objective of taking one alive achieved, there was no reason to spare the other who came at me with a roar. This one was no novice in warfare as I soon realised. His feints and parries revealed a true warrior, and I found myself forced into steady retreat until the voice of Osbald penetrated my concentration.

"The under-thrust, Lord Ecgwulf!"

My old thegn, a veteran of many such situations, spotted the weakness in the Dane's defence. How had I not noticed? It seemed obvious now he called it to me. With a dextrous twist of my arm and a dropping of the shoulder, I repeated the blow Osbald had taught me at twilight in Sondwic two years past. The surprised Dane howled, dropped, and, destined to die anyway, I dispatched him for the Valkyries to snatch his soul.

When the cheering died, I ordered the surviving Norseman to be pegged spread-eagled on the ground. This done, shrugging aside the thanks of the rescued ceorls, I shouted, "A bucket of water!" It appeared at once. Taking it from a wide-eyed girl, I sloshed the contents on the face of the pinioned man who, spluttering, regained consciousness.

I knelt beside him and in a loud, ringing voice, informed

him, "If you wish to stay alive, you will tell me who is your leader and where he lives."

The brave fool made to spit at me, which earned him a punch in the mouth and a split lip.

"Tell me what I want to know, or I will have those stakes replaced by four horses, I will whip the beasts myself."

To be torn limb from limb is not an appealing prospect and the effect of my words was to be seen in the wild eyes of the Dane.

His words came so unwillingly I could not understand them.

"Speak up, I ordered, else I shall do it!"

"Jarl Sigurd," he said, spitting blood – not towards me.

"Lord, Jarl Sigurd is based ten leagues to the west. I know of his encampment!" It was the man with the pitchfork.

"Can you lead us there?"

The man looked worried. "But, forgive me, Lord, you cannot attack Sigurd with so few men."

The painful grin of the captive Dane confirmed that to ride into Sigurd's camp meant certain death.

"A map will be enough. Can you do that?"

He could, but having no parchment in the farmstead, a pointed stick in the earth had to suffice. The directions were clear enough for us to find our way there. His map also included a vantage point to observe the Danes without being spotted ourselves. Confirmation of the accuracy of this suggestion came from the glare of the bound Viking. The glower drew Osbald's attention too.

"What about him?"

"Let the farmers decide!"

No sooner had I said the words than the pitchfork was driven into the stomach of the helpless victim.

I wondered if he could have been spared to work as a slave

on rebuilding the barn, these were days without mercy on both sides. The hatred ran too deep. I had seen enough of Viking devastation myself to make me hate the pagans.

I nodded without a word to the farmer and gave him my hand. Remounting, I called my men to follow the route sketched in the soil.

To gain the vantage point, we slew a lookout with a well-aimed arrow before his raised horn could blast a warning. From there, we studied the extent of Sigurd's encampment. I calculated he disposed of more than a hundred men, and Osbald agreed. An assault from the east seemed the best option, but it would have to be a battle, not a raid.

All this, we referred to Aethelred in Tame Weorth who, at once, decided to head the attack himself. Of course, he wanted me by his side, not only to lead him there but because to renounce the services of *the Dane-slayer* would have been an act of folly, though I mention it myself...

It was my first pitched battle. At last, I experienced the enervating wait in the shield wall. That blood-chilling moment of tension immediately before the battle commences is hard to convey. It is when the terrifying wave of attackers breaks on your resisting, knotted muscles, the air torn with enemy war cries and the sigh of falling weapons through the air. We destroyed the Danes and slew Jarl Sigurd that long, wearing, blood-drenched day, at great cost, making Mierce a safer place for its folk while enhancing my already burgeoning reputation as a warrior. But why is it that every time I swell with joy, events rear their heads to deflate me?

9

WINTAN-CAESTRE, OCTOBER, 898 AD

His name means 'wise elf,' and, of course, I'm obsessed with wisdom. I am given to thinking, the more responsibility a man has, the more of it he needs. And now, on the twenty-sixth day of the eighth month, the 'wise elf' died and left his people bereft at his passing. Not only the West Seaxa mourned King Alfred but all those who understood the meaning of greatness. Had he not defended his kingdom against the Vikings and overseen the conversion of their leader, Guthrun? He was a learned, merciful, and gracious ruler, is that not true? Education, justice, and the military were improved, and, without this, what a wretched life our people would have endured.

These thoughts filled my head as I rode to Wintan-caestre upon receiving the news. I sought to pay my respects at his tomb in the Minster but, above all, to meet with Edward and Aethelflaed to determine my future and that of my family.

I found a court rife with suspicion and whisperings when I reached West Seax. The death of Alfred did not leave a straightforward succession. Edward's cousin, Aethelwold, had a strong claim to the kingship as the son of Alfred's elder brother and predecessor, Aethelred. Aethelwold aetheling and his brother were still infants when their father the king died while fighting a Danish Viking invasion, so the throne passed to the king's younger brother Alfred.

The West Seax nobility were divided over who had the better claim. Even I, when I thought about it, considered Aethelwold's the more legitimate claim. But my sister being married to Edward tended to sway my decision.

In the confusion of what happened next, it is hard for me to say what occurred. Aethelwold cannot have gained enough support to raise an army against those in favour of Edward. Many nobles, for love of the late King, supported Edward's claim. Maybe they hoped the son would be as wise and strong as the father. Whatever the case, Aethelwold refused to accept Edward's lordship but rode instead to seize the royal residence at Wimborne. On hearing of this, Edward summoned me to his hall.

"Ecgwulf, dear brother, grim news! I need your sword in my service. Aethelwold aetheling has kidnapped my sister and taken her to Wimborne."

"What!"

"And he says he will live or die there. We march on Wimborne. My army gathers on the heights at Badbury, a league from his lair." There we rode to join Edward's forces, I savoured the prospect of another battle. We established camp, but, unknown to us, the most unexpected event happened during the night.

At first light, our army made to encircle the fortified royal palace, before completing the deployment, a solitary figure in armour rode out and made for King Edward. Had Aethelwold come to submit to, to parley, or to challenge the King? It was not so! Spears rose like bristles, and men nocked arrows as a precaution against a disloyal attack on the King. My hand strayed to the hilt of *Breath Stealer,* the rider halted three yards from us. Removing the helm, a cascade of blonde hair fell over the shoulders of the horseman. What am I saying? Horse*man?*"

"Hail, brother!" she said.

"Aethelflaed!" Edward cried and nudged his horse forward to take and kiss his sister's hand. "Where is the rebel, Aethelwold?" the King asked for an answer we all longed to hear.

"Gone! He fled in the night. Whither, I know not."

How on earth had he managed to pass by our sentries?

In fact, weeks elapsed before we learnt that the aetheling had fled to the Viking army in Northanhymbre. The Norsemen accepted him as king, swearing allegiance. My dissatisfaction at not fighting promised to be temporary. Aethelwold would likely head south with a host to fight for the West Seax throne.

How curious this was, my first encounter with Lady Aethelflaed. She looked at ease in armour, confirming the sundry tales of her martial prowess. One such tale will suffice. She, as a maid of fourteen, on her way to wed Aethelred of Mierce had organised and led her own escort, without fear, to repel a Danish ambush. I gazed at her in awe. She was not beautiful like my sister, but her countenance pleased me for its strength combined with femininity. She noticed my scrutiny, and her smile charmed me on the instant.

"You are Ecgwulf. I have heard much spoken about you."

"And most of it exaggerated, I doubt not," I said with false modesty.

"It is a pleasure to meet, at last." Her grin broadened to reveal even white teeth with a slight gap at the front.

"Let us go inside, brother. Dismiss the men. There will be no bloodshed *today*." The stress on the last word struck me as far-sighted and, perhaps because I wanted to believe it so, made her sound disappointed like me.

Eating honey cakes, quaffing mead, and conversation, for any normal man, is a more pleasant pastime than hacking and hewing at an enemy. I worried that my despondency at missing warfare might be a sign of madness. But Aethelflaed's words reassured me I was not alone in my derangement.

"It is a question of time before we fight with Aethelwold. We must make all arrangements to best secure your throne, brother. One or two people will have to be removed in West Seax." She accompanied this with flashing eyes and a gesture of drawing a finger across her throat.

"Above all," Edward said, "you must encourage Aethelred to strengthen Miercian defences against an invasion from Northanhymbre. I fear Aethelwold will have fled there. If not, where else?"

"My husband does not enjoy good health, but I shall attend to it. You may rely on me, Edward."

The king nodded in grateful acknowledgement.

"Of course, we do not know what success Aethelwold will have in raising an army. He might not come at all."

"And the sun may rise in the west!"

Such was Edward's certainty the Vikings would seize any pretext to invade Saxon-held lands.

Impatient to know what Edward had in mind for me, I hesitated to interrupt these important discussions.

"What do you think, Ecgwulf?"

Edward's knack of reacting to my thoughts always disconcerted me.

"Aethelwold is driven by rancour. He will not give up his attempt to usurp your throne. But what of me and of Ecgwynn? Will you not take her to Wintan-caestre now you are King?"

"And risk her life and those of her children?"

His reply shocked me, and I did not fail to notice he referred to the babes as *her* and not *their* offspring.

"But now King Alfred is gone, God rest his soul, where is the danger?"

"My father did not dispatch the murderers to Sondwic. Whoever did is still a threat and will for sure be a supporter of Aethelwold."

"Unless *he* sent them," Aethelflaed joined in.

"They will all be safer in Mierce under your protection. That's my last word on the matter."

"What about me?" I blurted.

"You must do what Father wanted. Fight for my sister. Know that you ever have my love and friendship, brother."

Thus, his decision sealed my fate. Quite how fateful it would be, Edward could not suspect. Nor was I to know how this particular inflexibility reflected his character, so worthy of succeeding his father. Edward was not studious like his father but surpassed him as a military leader.

I do not intend my tale to become a chronicle of battles against the Danes won and lost. They were seldom lost when I was involved, but the years after Alfred's death were remarkable for little else. The health of Aethelred, Lord of Mierce, continued to decline. Otherwise, there were two significant events. The first occurred in the following spring and was devastating for my family.

---

899 AD

KING EDWARD SAW FIT TO MAKE HIMSELF A MORE prestigious marriage by wedding the daughter of a mighty West Seax nobleman. I have no doubts about the strategic merits of his decision to marry, but what about poor Ecgwynn? What about her? Her heart was broken, and she never recovered. Can a woman die for love? She did – pining, not eating and dwelling in misery. I'm convinced the fatal blow came with the birth of Aelflaed's first son, Aelfweard.

Edward was decent enough to travel to Mierce for the funeral of Ecgwynn, and after the service, I had the opportunity to confront him. Understanding my raw feelings, he spoke with care.

"I feel for you, brother. Our loss is monstrous, ay, for both of us. We must talk about Athelstan."

"He's an orphan."

"Not while I'm alive."

"You recognise him?"

"The same old Ecgwulf! These matters are not so simple."

His wavy chestnut hair flailed into mine as Edward thrust his face close.

"I loved Ecgwynn," he hissed, "and I love Athelstan, which is why he must, as my father wished, become King of Mierce. Aethelred's health is poor, and he will not survive."

"Athelstan is still a young boy! Are you serious?"

"Never more so. You and Aethelflaed will tutor him in all things befitting a king. But beware the ambitions of my sister."

So, in the end, Edward and I parted on amicable terms whereas, when we met, I wanted to slay him. The grief lasted for years – my brotherly love for my sister was so deep – but I concentrated on the upbringing of Athelstan.

AUTUMN, 902 AD

THE NEW CENTURY BROUGHT ABOUT THE SECOND remarkable event. It found Aethelflaed well prepared. This outstanding leader, in the enforced absence of her husband, whose malady meant he spent more time abed than not, declared herself Lady of the Miercians. Her determination, bravery, and just nature won her the heartfelt enthusiasm of her people – and my love and loyalty.

Our spies warned us in good time of Aethelwold's return south in the autumn of the year of Our Lord, 901. He settled among the Vikings of Est Anglia. We made our men ready for the expected assault. The aetheling spent one year inducing the Est Anglian Vikings to break the peace and harry the kingdom of Mierce. The fortresses Aethelflaed had built proved redoubtable but their garrisons could not stop the devastation in the surrounding villages. The strongholds provided refuge for the populace, and Aethelwold and his Norsemen did not know how to deal with them. Thus, we sallied forth with our warriors and drove them into Wiltunscir. When Aethelwold and his forces crossed the Thames into Wessex and raided Braydon, King Edward pursued them with his army and harried Est Seax and Est Anglia. That is to say, all the Viking lands between the Dykes and the Ouse, as far north as the Fens.

Edward entrusted the men of Kent to me, a man who would lead them well. Who better than *the Dane-slayer?* – one of their own. I was preoccupied not to ravish the steadings in revenge but to chase the retreating army of Danes and Angles into their kingdom. King Edward was not eager to pursue the enemy over the confines because, as ever, his thoughts turned to Lunden. The town lay not so distant from the Est Anglian border, and he was loath to leave it too far behind him. I understood this because whoever held Lunden controlled the south of England.

My preoccupation was to destroy the Danes and slay King Eohric for his treason. That is what drove me on in pursuit, knowing the Danes would set an ambush at some point. The land and the weather favoured them in this. Est Anglia, criss-crossed by rivers, dykes, and ditches and a patchwork of marshes, was as near to a wilderness as was possible. The last month of the year upon us, the rain, the mists rising off the marshland, and the biting wind made the uniform greyness and the mud everywhere a nightmare. We dropped down from the low hills into this landscape. The plain afforded little natural cover. The foe knew our weakness since we became ever more detached from Edward's main army, intent on ravaging Eohric's lands rather than keeping up.

In these miserable conditions, I led my men to the River Use where the Roman bridge spanned it. Even my youthful impetuosity baulked at the thought of crossing there. I too would have set an ambush in that place. On the other side of the river, the ground rose higher. I would not lead my men to slaughter at a bridge so easy to defend. Instead, I sent scouts upriver where they found many Danish ships moored but more important, another bridge at a place called Eanulfsbirig. We went over there, and I discovered a formidable knoll to hold some eight-hundred yards from the wide river where it looped. On the hillock, there was a small cluster of trees, ideal to conceal men, and on either flank lay marsh. In front of us, a flooded ditch offered protection from a slithering foe. Over the Use, we were vulnerable, but this was better than marching straight to the enemy's choice of battlefield.

I chose a messenger to ride to King Edward, urging him to come to our position. Without his army, we were in mortal danger, so much stronger was the enemy. At least the small woodland provided us with kindling and logs. The days were shortening, and nightfall brought bitter cold. What would morning bring? The thought filled me with dread. It might become a race against time between the Danish advance and the arrival of Edward's army. Having passed the bridge, the

Danes could form their shield wall, but the deep flooded ditch gave some protection. It worried me they might skirt the marsh to attack us from the rear. My anxiety turned to desperation when the messenger returned with a pronouncement from Edward. We were to withdraw at once. He had no intention of coming to face the enemy. I chose to ignore his command. The Danes had to be fought even if it meant every last man of Kent shedding his lifeblood on the sodden Est Anglian earth. Edward sent more riders with the same message throughout the night and six times I defied him...I am a stubborn man, and now we were on our own.

10

BATTLE OF THE HOLME, EST ANGLIA
902 AD

I cannot relate the tale of the battle, yet I think about it often and never without tears. Of course, I have fought in many battles, and the telling is no problem, but this is different. Thanks to my stubborn refusal to withdraw that night, many comrades and friends breathed their last. Owing to the same decision, without exaggeration, the entire future of our folk changed.

If I and others of my men survived, it is also because Aethelflaed harried the Danes to the north of our battlefield. At the time, I wondered why the foe did not attack at once with their superior might. Later, I learnt the fear of the Lady of the Miercians at their backs was the reason. Their delay allowed Edward time to decide to gallop to our aid, but not until completely surrounded, and, hard-pressed, we lost so many men that we almost succumbed.

What I will relate is the grumbling prelude to the battle. How my warriors resented the long practice of the shield wall that I put them through! And yet, it paid off. My angry shouts and insults at those who could not keep the shields locked together brought dark mutters of resentment. Add to that my insistence on an alternation of axemen and swordsmen with training of the former to hook the enemy shields with their axe-heads to drag away their protection. This meant inculcating a different mentality: curbing the warrior's instinct to smash the axe-head down on an adversary's shield in a futile attempt to shatter it with one monstrous blow. They hated it, but it cost the foe dear. Once again, I was proved right!

When, with reluctance, I think back to that fateful day, it was the bloodiest of the engagements I have fought in; given I have lost count of them, it says a lot. Our shield wall discipline and the difficulty for the enemy to cross the slippery ditch in front helped us hold out beyond reasonable expectation.

One other thing I will take credit for is my slaying of Aethelwold. Or more accurately, from wherever God has decided he should now reside, he should claim the merit for his own death. The aetheling sought me out. Quite rightly, I believe, he wanted to put an end to my existence there in the midst of my men. As he saw it, my demise would break our resistance and win the day, although he knew my reputation as a warrior. Men do not stop to weigh up these things in the heat of battle. The slightest hesitation can be fatal. So, on he came, shouting oaths at me, trying to provoke me into an unwise rage – another potentially fatal error in the circumstances and one I would never make. I stayed calm, seething inside, and took the full might of his onslaught on my shield. I promised to spare the details of gore and slaughter, so suffice to say, he wounded me, but I slew him, and his death changed the course of events.

The demise of Aethelwold consolidated Edward's kingship – as I pointed out to him when, afterwards, he sought to reprove me for my disobedience. I believe, to this day, the battle also marked a turning point, although the change in the tide of power was not seen at once. But it is no coincidence that

Edward and Aethelflaed and I drove the Danes out of Mierce allowing Edward to gain control of the whole land. But that is a tale yet to be told.

On that terrible day, the Ealdormen Sigewulf and Sige-helm, the thegn Eadwold, and abbot Cenwulf were among our other important and grievous losses. But the enemy lost more men than we did; owing to Edward's tardy arrival, the slaughter was horrendous. Apart from Aethelwold, the aetheling, the souls of King Eohric of Est Anglia, Brihtsige son of the aetheling Beornoth, Ysopa, and Oscetel, departed this life.

There was little respite after the battle of the Holme. The Vikings continued to do what they always did: raid, rape, and plunder in Mierce. It went on for four years – spent in strength-ening my reputation as *the Dane-slayer* until King Edward decided to pay off the Danes, Est Angles, and Northanhym-brians to stop their harrying. He did this at Tiddingford – something I cannot condone – but I'm getting ahead of myself.

Indulge me while I go back to the construction of the new Minster at Wintan-caestre. I think Edward wanted to mark his ascension as an establishment of the line of Alfred – a state-ment of sorts. Construction began in 901 close to the old Minster, and when the splendid building was consecrated, he had the remains of King Alfred laid to rest therein. This would bear on subsequent events I wish to relate. Edward granted the land on condition that prayers were said at the monastery every day for himself, his father, and his ancestors. Alfred's wife Ealh-swith was buried at the New Minster on her death in 902. So, it was not by the sword alone that Edward's kingship became consolidated.

In Mierce, meanwhile, distractions caused by Danish raids aside, I spent all my available time training Athelstan in the use of arms. I believe that if you begin to learn early, younger than I did, the better you assimilate. Athelstan started to wield a practice sword against me at the tender age of seven. We were both learning. I, to teach one so young, to realise that his main opponents were his pride and fierce desire to please. He, to build enough strength and courage to endure the harsh treatment.

The boy came of excellent stock and made rapid progress, but Time cannot be cheated; its dues must be paid. Every age in childhood brings different problems; the next one I had to overcome was frustration. The lad yearned to be a renowned warrior like his uncle, and I saw tears of vexation roll down his cheeks. Far worse, so did Aethelflaed, who had strolled out to gauge his progress, and she did not have the sense to stay silent. The Lady of the Miercians, ruler, all but in name, wore a sword at her waist at all times. This was befitting of a warrior queen.

"Athelstan, are you crying like a babe?" she mocked.

Distracted, Athelstan let up his guard and I 'slew' him with my wooden sword.

The taunting laughter that followed annoyed me too, but I loved Aethelflaed and bit my tongue to stifle a reprimand. Athelstan, instead, flushed bright red as a fourteen-year-old will when scoffed at.

"If you find it so funny, Aunt, step up and face me, if you're not afraid!"

"A stripling like you isn't man enough to give *me* a fight! I'm used to slaying Vikings. You still stink of your mother's milk!"

What a crass thing to say! She should never have touched that particular nerve. Before I could intervene, Athelstan flew at her and landed a clout of his wooden sword on her arm as she protected her head. The look of hatred on the youngster's face shocked me. He had never glared at me in such a way.

Aethelflaed howled in pain. It was a wonder the limb was not broken.

"Come on, witch!"

Her sword flashed out in an arc of steel – a real keen-edged blade. This taunting had flown out of control. How could I stand by while my beloved nephew was cut to pieces for his rashness and mordant tongue? I rushed to retrieve *Breath Stealer* and with a strenuous lunge managed to interpose the blade between the boy's head and Aethelflaed's weapon.

"I don't need your aid, Uncle," yapped the ungrateful pup.

"Do you mean to kill the boy, Aethelflaed?"

My words seemed to wake her like a bucketful of icy water hurled at the face of a sleeper.

"Of course not," she said, "but he must learn manners."

"You cannot fight a boy armed with a practice sword with that!"

"I'm not a boy anymore!"

"Shut up!"

"Then give me your pretend weapon, and we'll see how much of a man he is."

I admit, maybe I was wrong, I gave her the false sword with alacrity. Why I did, I'll never know. I should have put an end to the nonsense there and then. After all, it was my training session, but I reckon the sheer relief of removing Aethelflaed's real sword from the confrontation explains it.

The Lady of the Miercians was carrying a very sore arm, which might account for the evenness of the contest. I had seen her covered in gore, in battle, slaying men three times Athelstan's size. He, instead, driven by pride and rage and, modesty apart, trained by an expert, gave as good as he received. Maybe Aethelflaed's self-regard stirred her at a certain point. Whatever, she redoubled her efforts, and watching her graceful movements, her grain-coloured hair flying about her face, captivated me. I half-longed to be her adversary in the place of my nephew.

Anyway, with her full-blooded effort came success. She drove Athelstan off balance and thrust the practice sword hard at his throat, robbing him of breath and forcing him to his knees. Her face was a picture. She threw the wooden sword to the ground in disgust with herself and sobbed. When Athelstan's breathing returned in gulps, he started to weep out of humiliation. So, I had two of them in tears. To my credit, my first concern was my nephew. I went to him and hauled him to his feet.

"Congratulations, warrior," I said, and I meant it because not many adversaries survived so long in the face of Aethelflaed's wrath. She was as fierce a fighter as the shield maiden Freydis of the Viking tales. I struggled to catch his muttered reply. "But I lost to a woman!" The humiliation seared at his pride.

"No ordinary woman," I said it with a deliberately loud voice, so she should hear, "but a goddess!"

Aethelflaed looked up, her face wet, and favoured me with a weak smile.

"We are even now," she said. "I'm sorry I mocked you, Athelstan, you are, indeed, a real warrior, one who merits a sword of his own. I shall gift you one."

So spoke the Aethelflaed I loved.

My nephew shrugged off my embrace and flew to his aunt, so happy was he at the thought of having his personal weapon. He flung his arms around her and buried his head in her golden locks. How I envied him that moment!

"What's more," she said, "the next time the Danes muster the courage to raid our lands, I will take you with us to repel them. But after last year's defeat..."

"Promise, Aunt Aethelflaed!"

"I give you my word."

So, the day ended on a better note than I might have hoped. Yet, I had my doubts about the wisdom of her decision. Was Athelstan ready? After seven years of instruction, I had little left to impart. Only Time could give him the strength he needed to be a complete warrior.

---

911 AD

EVENTS MARCH ON RELENTLESSLY HAND IN HAND WITH Time. Later in the year, Ealdorman Aethelred's suffering came to an end, and he passed away. Aethelflaed did not need to assume control of Mierce; she already had it. However, Edward sent his men to take possession of Lunden and Oxford until then still, in name, Miercian. No matter, Aethelflaed's loyalty to her brother was unswerving.

Thanks to her new fortresses and the massive victory at Wednesfield, the year before, where thousands of Northanhymbrians perished under our swords, Edward could sleep easy. But he did not sit idle. Like his sister, he built strongholds. In particular, one at Witham where he took the submission of the Est Seaxa. Aethelflaed constructed two others at Tame Weorth and at Stafford, where she founded the burh. These protected the northwest borders of Mierce, meaning peace and a longer time for Athelstan to grow into sturdy manhood.

11

TAME WEORTH, 911 AD

"You're afraid of women, aren't you?"
I blurted, "No, I'm not!" and fled from
Aethelflaed's presence with her mocking words, "I say you
are," ringing in my ears accompanied by her scornful laugh.
My escape proved her right. I found a quiet arbour in the
garden to think. There, I sat on a stone bench next to a thick
quince shrub. Alone, in that secluded bower, my thoughts
whirled around ways to satisfy my lust and show her what
kind of man I was.

Was she right about me? Aethelflaed's suggestive smile and
step toward me had made me flee like a startled hare. The back-
ward step I took that provoked her comment came from
instinct. As such, I had to understand my behaviour. Unlike the
men I knew, Edward for example, who could not stay away
from maids, I did not seek them out. Why? I do not care for
men: not in that way.

Athelstan, who does not keep the company of wenches or
ladies, has achieved more than me. The serving maid he took
after our victory came to mind. I have never lain with a woman.

I glared at the heart-shaped leaves of the quince. *Heart*, was there ought wrong with mine?

I like women as creatures. A shapely wench pleases my eye. Why did I never make a move? I had enough chances. I flatter myself I have good looks, though my countenance is not beautifully sculpted like that of my late sister. Ay, Ecgwynn, she's the root of the problem. When I close my eyes and pray for her soul every night, I see her lovely face as if she stood in front of me. My love for her is deep. Yet it was never more than chaste and brotherly. Can it be that no other woman will ever take her place?

A linnet alighted on the shrub in a flurry of feathers and began to warble its lyrical song. The speckled, red-breasted bird, so timid, minded not my presence. I did not move a muscle for fear of scaring it away. Ridiculous fancy insisted it had assumed the blithe spirit of Ecgwynn come to comfort me with this exquisite trill.

My love for my sister was pure...ay...but obsessive, in truth. However, I never used to touch her out of lust, nothing to arouse the wrath of the Church or of my family. The problem, I recognised, was another, it resided in my head. No woman could obscure Ecgwynn or take her place. Not that she had always responded to my affection with sweetness. I remember she often scolded me. At this moment, the little bird winged away and left me with my regrets.

Why had Aethelflaed's eyes settled on me? Out of respect? I did nothing to disguise my liking for her. I dwelt on the Lady of the Miercians and found myself with a stupid smile on my face. Was I falling in love? Why her?

The answers came at once. She remained the one woman I respected with all my heart. Not because she was a worthy warrior, like me, although it did set her apart from all others. I laughed at the thought of Ecgwynn wearing a sword, let alone wielding one! There was more to Aethelflaed than that; her personality impressed all she met. Her Miercians loved her for the peace she gained for them in combat, but it was her rational manner, combining justice and charity, that won the people over. I also admired her character.

I rose from the bench, a decision taken. I needed to return to Aethelflaed to demonstrate to her and myself how wrong she was. Did sanity desert me? It seemed to me the painted carved figures on the doorpost of the entrance to the hall sneered in unison with my curled lip at the thought of *the Dane-slayer* with a fear of women. It made me laugh. A servant carrying logs gazed at me to acknowledge my madness. I glared at him, and he hurried over to the hearth.

"Someone ought to gather in the quinces before the first frosts arrive," I said to Aethelflaed, who looked up from leafing through the pages of a document. My words caused the mocking sparkle in her eyes on seeing me changed to wonderment.

"Since when have you been interested in plants, Ecgwulf?"

I confronted her, "How little you know about me. Why else would you err in misguided accusation."

"Accusation?"

"You accused me of being afraid of women." I gave her a disparaging look.

"Oh, that! It's true, I say you *are*!"

A mischievousness shone in her eye, and she ran the tip of her tongue along her upper lip.

"I have come back to prove you wrong."

"How do you mean to do that?" She thrust her weight on one leg so that her hip jutted toward me and leant forward in an attractive act of provocation. Aethelflaed set my pulse racing. This was a new experience.

"Put me to the test," I croaked.

She glanced around the hall.

"Come, follow!"

She led me across the hall and into her private chamber. If asked to describe her bedchamber, I would be unable to do so. I had eyes only for the golden-haired Aethelflaed. She unbuckled her sword and hung it over the bedhead. Her teasing voice came to me over her shoulder. "*Dane-slayer*, you have made it this far. What do you intend to do next?"

In truth, I did not know, but the scornful tone inflamed me in the wrong way, and I treated her as an enemy, seizing her arm and dragging her to me. My absurd intention was to push my face into hers so that my eyes glared into hers.

She misunderstood the gesture and pressed her lithe body close to mine so that before I could muster a scowl, her tongue pressed between my lips. Remember, I had never kissed a woman other than my mother and sister in a chaste manner on the cheek. New sensations spread from our eager mouths to the rest of my body. My head spun and, losing my balance, I clung on to Aethelflaed, hauling her down on the bed. Such was the pathetic start to my romantic adventure. Sheer luck mistaken for boldness aided my cause. The Lady of the Miercians, my Aethelflaed, mistook me for the assured, dominant lover I was not. Not at all a passive woman, she played her part in the proceedings, and suffice it to say, I lay with a woman for the first time.

Remembering to show no insecurity, I held my golden-haired conqueror in a close and tender embrace.

"I was wrong," she murmured with an infuriating smug smile on her face.

"About?"

"*You*, my love," she purred, stroking the war-hardened muscle of my upper arm. "I can say without fear of contradiction, you are *not* afraid of women. Forgive my taunt, but it served a purpose. It spurred you into action. I feared you would never make a move!"

I can't recall what I muttered, but it prolonged our love-making. Later, in the warm afterglow, I knew I had found the love of my life. She warned how we must be discreet. She could not tolerate gossip about her private life. The affection of her people was more important than her fondness for me. She tried to make me understand. Since she was a widow, I saw no obstacle to an eventual union. The idea of taking Aethelred's place as Lord of the Miercians had a certain appeal. No hurry. First, we must develop a relationship. This is what I told myself on that first heady afternoon of love. One thing was crystalline on that intoxicating occasion, *Aethelflaed* was had no fear of men! I would have a mighty task to set our blossoming rapport on an equal footing.

1 2

912-917 AD

The next few years, Aethelflaed and Edward built fortresses as a counter to Danes, Vikings, rebel Angles, and the Wealisc devastating our land wherever it could not be defended. Amid these violent circumstances, young Athelstan forged his skills as a warrior. Looking back on this period, I consider this successful transition from youth to man on the part of Athelstan to have been the reason for his later greatness. It also accounts for the wicked plots to take his life, almost as though the number of enemies a princeling makes is the measure of his valour.

I shall not linger on what happened in these years except for where they are important to the tale of Athelstan. To commence, Aethelflaed, glorying in her increasing reputation and power, blocked the advance of the Est Anglian Danes. They, however, kept us busy in the following year, 913. I say 'us' because against my better judgement (which for once proved wrong) Aethelflaed upheld her promise and took the youthful Athelstan into battle. First, she presented him with a sword fit for a king, complete with bejewelled belt and scab-

bard. Not wanting to be left out of Athelstan's exuberant celebrations, I dug out Alfred's gifts from their place of
safekeeping.

This was Athelstan's eighteenth spring, he had grown into
a fine iron-muscled fellow. When he was younger, I feared he
might become a priest since his nose was forever buried in a
book. I blamed this on his aunt, whose love of reading I never
understood. But I need not have worried, for every hour of
reading, he took a turn of the sand-glass at weapon practice. I
grew to care for him as though he were my own son. That is
why I wish to recount his tale.

The thirteenth year of the new century saw Athelstan slay
his first Viking. The Norsemen brought a raiding party from
Ledecestre into Mierce before veering off towards Lunden. We
caught them after they had killed many men at Hook Norton.
Having taken much booty, they rode back over the border
where they met with another band of Danes and joined forces,
determined to ride on the settlement at Leagrave. The local
men found out about their plan and gathered into a sizeable
force, which caused our arrival, designed to warn them, to be
greeted with irritating mirth. Much merriment was caused by
us revealing something they were privy to. But it was no
laughing matter, they were keen enough to unite my two-score
men to their number.

The battle, not much more than a skirmish in terms of dura-
tion, such was the efficacy of our well-laid ambush, was a short,
sharp slaughter. Before it began, I insisted on Athelstan staying
close to me. I figured, in this way, I should better protect him
during his first taste of warfare. But when I shouted the order to
break cover, the scamp leapt up so fast and sprinted at twice my
speed toward the mounted Vikings. It's a wonder he didn't
leave his hide to the scavengers that day. Instead, I marvelled at
how he unseated his chosen target with his spear and finished

the writhing Norseman with his new sword. Valiant and head-strong as you like, but it is thanks to his uncle that his head is still on his shoulders. I managed to intercept a vicious blow aimed at his unguarded back.

An oncoming comrade of the slain man delivered it, but the solid ash pole of my spear blocked the arc of the scything downward strike. The jarring effect on the rider numbed his sword hand and sent his weapon spinning to the ground. Before I reacted, Athelstan, warned by the sound, spun round and, like a hunting hound, leapt at the dangling arm to tug the warrior off his horse. I incurred my nephew's rage by skewering the Viking with my spear. I could not risk the heavier man bettering the agile but lighter youth.

The ungrateful whelp had the nerve to reprimand me for *'depriving me of my kill, Uncle.'* After a battle, I'm not given to words, but he provoked them that day. A man must learn to fight with his wits about him. I gave him a severe reprimand. In return, he sulked all the ride back to Leagrave. There, feasting and sharing of the recovered booty was planned.

I'm unsure whether our hosts were more delighted to celebrate the victory or to have King Alfred's grandson as a guest among them. I'm not sure, I think Athelstan not only killed his first Viking that day but also took his first maid. That suspicion came to me when I saw his eyes follow a fair servant everywhere she went in the hall. Their exchanged glances and smiles and the girl's blushes spoke to me of a growing attraction between them. So, when distracted by conversation to my left, I turned to Athelstan to involve him and found his seat empty, my suspicion grew. It became a certainty when I saw no trace of the wench in the hall.

"Where did you get to?"

Thus, I greeted him on his return.

"Nature called, Uncle."

"That's a strange expression for it!"

"What do you mean?"

He looked as if he might float to the rafters so inflated with pride was he.

"No man I know takes that long to piss, none of them ever returns with that sort of grin on his smug face. A piss is only a piss, after all."

The beam grew wider, and the rascal asked for more ale.

"You'll have a right thirst on you now!"

We whiled away a pleasant evening in friendly banter followed by a rousing song, I must mention the fine melody about the exploits of a certain *Dane-slayer*. By God, that brought the whelp back down to earth with a bump.

He badgered me. Was it true, this and that? It was all I could get from him for the rest of the night before we surrendered to sleep by the glowing hearth. Just as well, after what I had seen in the afternoon: I needed all his respect if I were to teach him how to remain alive.

---

914 AD

THERE WAS TIME FOR THAT BECAUSE THE DANES STAYED quiet through the winter and so did his aunt Aethelflaed until the spring. I am a quick learner, as Osbald will agree, but Athelstan was no slouch. Later, we would be grateful to each other we had both learnt our lessons well. The spring, at least the first part, was peaceful too, but in June there came a double threat to Mierce. The Danes of the Five Boroughs resumed their raiding, and Aethelflaed marched to quell them. Almost at the same time, news came of a Danish fleet sailing from off Brittany. These Vikings sailed up into the Saefern estuary headed by two jarls, Ohter and Hroald, who led them to ravage into Wealas and along the coast. Thence they drove into Herefordscir. But the men of Hereford and Glevcaestre and the nearest fortresses in Mierce met them. Aethelflaed spared Athelstan and me with a force of fifty warriors to join them while she took the credit for slaughtering the Est Anglian Danes.

By now, my fame as *the Dane-slayer* preceded me, meaning men were keen and willing to follow me into battle. Thus, command of our forces was thrust upon me. I will not elaborate on our victory. What I will say is that Athelstan saved my skull from an axe-head while I was dispatching another Viking. He threw his hand seax into the face of my would-be slayer with his left hand whilst crossing blades with another, sword in his right. I have never been more proud or grateful. That seax finished in the eye of the enemy warrior, not bad for a cack-handed throw!

For the rest of the battle, my tactics worked thanks to the superior discipline of our men. That day, we slew Jarl Hroald and Ohter's brother. The Vikings, seeing those among their leaders fall, fled to a fortified encampment they had built by the Saefern. There we besieged them, battering our swords on our shields until they sent men out to treat with us. I spoke for us all and agreed to take hostages and a promise to leave in exchange for their miserable skins.

King Edward arrived, to his dismay, too late for the battle. Athelstan greeted his father with a sullen face, which only cheered when I decanted his fighting skills to the King. I reckon the lad felt betrayed by his sire and resentful of his mother's treatment. If so, it passed as he poured out the tale of the seax-throwing to his delighted parent who stepped over and embraced the young man.

"Thank you, son, *for saving my right arm.*" Those were his

words! *Me*, his right arm! Followed by, "...and bless you for helping drive the Vikings away from my kingdom."

Family reunion and flattery over, King Edward made arrangements to station men along the south bank of the Saefern. He, wisely, I believe, did not trust the promises of Norsemen, especially those of one who had lost his brother and close friends in battle. But he was right because Ohter broke the peace by raiding inland to Watchet and later to Porlock.

We caught them both times and inflicted on them the heavy losses they deserved. Driven back to the River Saefern, they took their ships the short distance to Steepholme Isle in the Channel. King Edward decided not to man a fleet to destroy them, considering their reduced number made them much less of a threat. These battles, though, served a significant purpose. I no longer worried about the safety of Athelstan in combat. Now it was a case of worrying for his opponents!

To complete the tale of Ohter, he took his men to raid in Dyfed and thence to Ireland, probably to lick his wounds over the winter. And I wish to be as short with the events that followed. In 915, Aethelflaed built fortresses at Chirbury to protect the border with Powys and at Rumcofan and Weard-burh to face the River Mersey. In the following year, Edward constructed a fortress in Maldon.

The seasons come and go while men do their worst to upset the harmony of life granted by the Creator. In the same 916, the Wealisc slew the innocent abbot Ecgberht and his companions on the sixteenth day of June. Incensed, three days later, Aethelflaed sent Athelstan and me into Wealas to destroy the settlement at Brecenanmere. There, in this pretty lakeside stronghold, I was deprived of my senses by a Wealisc shield driven under my jaw. It is the first and, I hope, the last time I missed a battle. Afterwards, it took three days before I could speak or eat food.

Athelstan marched around with his chest puffed out like a proud cockerel. I could not talk, but I heard the tales of how he stood over me and slew any of the Wealisc who dared come near to finish us both. As if this was not enough for me to bear, my men insisted on finishing the tale of the day. The battle over, Athelstan completed the task entrusted to him by the Lady of the Miercians and burned the settlement to the ground. He also captured the king's wife and thirty-three other prisoners: a fine haul to negotiate a ransom. With a leer, wink, and a nudge, one of the storytellers suggested that Athelstan had 'comforted' the queen in her distress. I wouldn't have put that past the scamp!

My pounding headache would not let me listen to any more of this nonsense, and I gave instructions that I was not to be disturbed, particularly by Athelstan.

Back in Tame Weorth, I endured the mockery of Aethelflaed. I loved her, but she had this annoying side to her character. In brief, she praised Athelstan's victory to the stars and consigned my part in it to the pigsties.

When our paths crossed, I mentioned the risk he had run in battle and how he still had much to learn.

"Fear not, Uncle, the risks are slight since I have such a great teacher."

"Remember, Nephew, your last mistake is always your greatest teacher," I snapped, and he looked at me askance. I mention this to explain, in spite of the high regard in which Athelstan was now held within and without Mierce, his greatest enemy was his overconfidence. His burgeoning reputation also placed him in increased peril.

13

TAME WEORTH, 917 AD

What Aethelflaed had in mind, I had no idea. That it involved something important became clear as she hurried about the Royal Palace with a determined air and no time for me. When three Wealisc kings arrived with their retinues, banners streaming, I felt compelled to ask everyone close to the Lady what was happening. Nobody, not counsellors, maids, Athelstan, or bishops, knew what she planned. From the north came the kings of Strathclyde, Bernicia, and the Scottas with their followers. The overcrowded town, teeming with people whose weird way of talking remained incomprehensible to me, no longer seemed like home.

Luckily, I did not have long to wait in these circumstances before Aethelflaed called me to a witan. All would become clear at the council meeting. The crowded hall made this so different from our previous meetings. Six kings from beyond the confines of Mierce and their own counsellors crammed in with the usual gathering of bishops, ealdormen, and aethelings.

Aethelflaed, a regal figure, although in name not a queen, arose wearing her inseparable sword, the bejewelled scabbard flashing in defiance of the dim light in the hall. The force of her personality drew all eyes to her and silenced the clamour in the room. Like me, every man in there hung on her words.

"Kings, lords, bishops, I have invited you here today for one reason only. I have decided to put an end to the Vikings..."

So outrageous seemed this declaration to me who worshipped her, I understood the instant commotion it provoked. Some minutes passed before order returned and she continued, "...the Norse scourge has troubled our people for too long. We must stamp out their pillaging and slaughtering."

The King of Strathclyde rose and waited to speak. A tilt of her blonde head and he proceeded to ask, "Lady, how do you propose to do that?"

Her smile might have melted ice. But she needed more than charm. She had to find a convincing argument.

"Half the battle is won, Sire, before we attack. To bring together the might of the north, Mierce and Wealas is enough to smite terror into the heart of the stoutest jarl. Speaking of which, I intend to strike at the very heartland of the Viking possessions here in Angle territory. Take Deoraby, and the other boroughs will fall. My brother Edward has control of the south. His mighty fortresses stood firm against every Viking assault. Swear to join me in this, and you have my word, the end of the bane that afflicts our lands."

The debate raged as fierce as a Viking raiding party's wrath, but the Lady of the Miercians stood tall and won the day. By the time the meeting dispersed, she had extracted promises of alliance from the kings present and the support of her own ealdormen with a promise of warriors and money.

I sought out Athelstan and found he shared my excitement at the prospect of war. When our allies arrived from their far-flung kingdoms, we would march on the Viking stronghold straddling the Derwent.

"Can we rely on the Scottas and the Wealisc, Uncle?"

"They hate the Vikings as much or, I dare say, more than we do, Athelstan. They see that if we take Deoraby, we cripple them. At last, someone means to take decisive action against the bastards! And you and I, Athelstan, will lead the assault."

A feral growl issued from my nephew's throat and his fists closed tight. At that moment, I realised what a slaying machine I had helped to create. Athelstan's eyes flashed. "How long do you think before the Scottas arrive?"

In his impatience, he had chosen the most distant of our allies.

"Give them one more moon, I'd say. So much the better, the weather will be kinder by then."

"But what kind of fighters are they?"

I had fought against the Wealisc but never the Scottas, I shrugged. "If their speech is aught to go by, they'll be damned hard to beat."

Athelstan, the young fool, took my throwaway remark seriously. "Splendid! Then we'll raze Deoraby to the ground."

I was not so sure. To walk straight into the wolf's lair did not strike me as an easy task, far from it.

I changed my mind, of course, riding at the head of the largest host I had ever seen assembled. Owing to its size, we sacrificed the advantage of surprise. The Vikings were ready for us and came streaming out of the gate to their town to form a long shield wall. On the journey there, we had supposed they would remain sheltered behind the walls. Now, as we faced the enemy, another problem arose. I started shouting orders only to be countermanded by Aethelflaed, imposing her strong character.

"Sister," I said, and she scowled, I had never called her that before, "we must try to outflank them. Let us divide our forces into two arms to encircle them."

I could see she wanted to refuse, but good sense prevailed under the wheat-coloured hair.

"But I will lead the centre," she insisted.

I nodded. The Wealisc with their strange ponies took the left flank, while Athelstan and I joined the kings from the north on the right. There, we were to find what ferocious fighters the Scottas were, but not one of them slew the number Athelstan dispatched, while I claimed more than my nephew. We caught the Vikings in a vice and Aethelflaed overwhelmed the centre. Their defensive walls were the undoing of the Danes. Pressed back, trapped, they could not flee. The slaughter was the most atrocious I ever saw – a tremendous victory! Despite this, Aethelflaed's joy was tempered by her sorrow at the loss of four of her beloved thegns.

The Lady of the Miercians now exerted all her authority. Although the conquerors desired to sack, pillage, and rape within the quaking settlement, she would have none of it. As she outstared the King of Strathclyde, I feared the worst – another battle between allies for plunder. Aethelflaed calmed the turbulent spirits by promising her new friends silver and gold before they left the kingdom. She argued that she would tax the Danes to recoup her expenses. Moreover, she declared, "I aim to restore the old borders of Mierce, wherein all men may farm or pursue a trade in peace."

She thought back to the golden age of Kings Aethelbald and Offa. I kept silent but feared this dream was beyond her powers to achieve. How right I was, but not in the way I imagined. In fact, the first thing that occurred during our feasting in celebration inside the walls of Deoraby surprised us all. Guards called our attention to a group of Danish riders, a raven banner streaming over their heads. News of our crushing victory resounded throughout the Danelaw and here came a delegation from Ledecestre to submit the borough to the shield-maiden of Mierce.

Two days later and into Deoraby rode a scarred warrior dressed Viking-style, his skull shaven to the crown from which hung down a thong-bound tail of hair. Blue inked symbols tattooed the skin of his head.

"Lady Aethelflaed," he said in a rough version of our tongue, "I come from Jorvik," which I knew as Eoforwic, "King Ragnall sends this as a sign of his submission." A fist unclenched to reveal a splendid ring of dazzling beauty, flashing ruby red. What ruler would have resisted such a gift? Aethelflaed nigh on leapt out of her seat to take and slip the precious gem on her slender finger. She turned it to catch the light in front of her face.

"Tell King Ragnall that we accept his generous gift and to expect our emissary before the moon is new."

Thinking about this development, I understood how wise the Viking king had been. Deira, after the victory at Deoraby, would not have accepted anything less than surrender from the occupiers of its former capital. Our combined force was awesome; none of the kings and jarls wished to risk incurring the fate of Deoraby. Taking advantage of the vast number of men at her disposal, Aethelflaed ordered the strengthening of the fortifications there. What a debt the folk of Angle-land owe to the vision of this remarkable woman!

In my lifetime, never had the Vikings been so weakened and the English so strong. We returned to Tame Weorth in triumph, paid off our allies, and looked forward to a brighter future. But in my experience, whenever things look to have taken a turn for the better, expect them to get worse.

14

THE KINGDOM OF ALBA, 917 AD

King Constantin greeted an invitation to make the long journey south to an urgent meeting hosted by Aethelflaed, the Lady warrior of the Miercians, with mixed reactions. Curious to meet the famed daughter of King Alfred, he was also reluctant to leave his homeland in troubled times. His western borders were more secure with his brother, Dyfn-wal, installed as King of Strathclyde, but the menace of the Norsemen loomed once more.

Their devastations in Ireland he considered too close for liking. Thanks to this Miercian noblewoman, the Viking fleet suffered defeat a few days past. She sent Saxon ships led by an ealdorman from Kent, named Ecgwulf, to confront them. The King's brow furrowed, he did not know this Ecgwulf but how he would like to clasp his hand for obtaining a victory that helped him sleep at night.

He was under no illusions the threat to the north was over and this, more than other considerations, made him accept the Lady's bidding. His son, Ildulb, would look after Alba in his absence but with a wary eye open for enemies within the king-dom, not those beyond the confines.

The Norsemen had not forgotten their defeat to Constantin in 904. The Viking leader, slain at his hands, Imair, had several sons, each keener than the other to avenge their father. Two of these savage young men, Sihtric and Ragnall, were most likely devastating a settlement in Ireland as he pondered. Constantin shuddered and took his decision. He would travel south with select warriors of his household, his portable altar, and the *Breccbennach*. So well-accompanied what harm could come to him?

The journey through Northanhymbre and into Mierce opened up a new world to Constantin. The fertile lands of Mierce appeared very different from the rugged terrain of his homeland. It was of great interest to him how far he had trav-elled to reach Tame Weorth. His cunning shrewdness told him that King Edward, whose royal vill lay farther still to the south would hesitate to take an army as far as Alba. Nobody could rule over so vast a territory. Confidence in this made his bargaining position stronger.

The time had come to meet the Lady of the Miercians: a woman who preferred the sword to a needle! What kind of woman might she be? He was about to find out. Aethelflaed strode into the hall to greet her visitors. Beside Constantin stood his nephew, Owain of Strathclyde, who had succeeded his father to the throne of that kingdom. Neither man cut an elegant figure as he gaped at their hostess. Her deportment, sword at her side, and demeanour belonged to a queen. Her presence and charm compensated for her lack of beauty, she remained a woman who would turn any man's head. Her long golden tresses hinted at wheat, molten gold, and amber as rays of sunlight streaming through the window played across them.

Realising the poor figure he cut by staring, Constantin

recovered to greet the Lady. Pleasantries exchanged, she tended to their needs after a long journey and invited them to dinner that night at her table in this same Hall. His eye strayed to the emblem of Mierce hanging on the wall to his right. A simple design, to his liking, no ferocious beast, no rampant dragon, but a plain yellow cross on a blue ground. She followed his gaze; there was regret in her voice. "The banner of a once-proud kingdom," she sighed. "Times change, but the valour of the Miercians is immutable."

"Much is spoken of your courage, Lady," Constantin made an attempt at gallantry because the woman pleased him."

Not one to be easily flattered, Aethelflaed fixed him with a level gaze, touched the hilt of her sword, and said, "I can hold my ground in battle."

Her sober tone carried more menace than a threat.

"Remind me not to argue with the Lady." Constantin grinned at Owain who risked a little laugh.

"I prefer to think our views will accord well, King Constantin," she said with a winsome smile. "But come, you must be weary after your long journey. A rest and refreshment are in order." She clapped, and servants hastened over. A few crisp commands and they took her guests to comfortable quarters.

Washed and changed, Constantin emerged to carry beakers of wine into his nephew's room. One he thrust into the younger man's hand. "Here try this, it's good. What do you think of the Lady Aethelflaed?"

"She might not be all she's vaunted to be with that sword. I'll wager my axe would soon put an end to her bragging."

"I don't think she bragged, and you make sure to keep such thoughts to yourself this evening, or you'll reckon with me!" Constantin thrust his fierce visage into that of his nephew.

"Uncle! I do believe you have a weakness for the Lady."

"And I'm thinking you have a death wish, laddie!"

99

The two of them had always been close. Owain took a step back, shocked, but the older man melted the ice.

"Come, drink of this brew; it's a marvel! Let's end this stupidity." He wrapped an avuncular arm over the other's shoulder. "Remember, Owain, it's to our advantage to play the perfect guests here. I must have a barrel of this wine brought to Alba."

"Do you think they make it here?"

"Shouldn't think so; it'll be imported from warmer climes."

"I'll ask about it when we eat."

"That's more like it."

Wisely, they drank up and went to lie their aching bones on their respective beds.

The hall resounded to jovial conversation, laughter, and exclamations. Constantin, still wearied by his journey, sat and studied his fellow guests. Listening attentively rather than joining in the exuberant banter, he learnt that three of his companions at the high table were kings in their own right. One, from Powys, shared a border with Mierce. The other two came from farther afield, Britons from different parts of Wealas.

Amid the unfamiliar faces, Constantin caught the eye of Ealdred who flashed him a smile. They were neighbours, as Ealdred's Northanhymbrian lands bordered his own. Of more interest to the King of the Scottas was the conversation of the Lady of Mierce. She did not betray the reason behind this gathering but seemed intent on examining the relationships existing among the rulers present. When Aethelflaed, at last, turned her attention to him, it was to probe the state of his dealings with Ealdred and the Bernicians. King Constantin regarded Ealdred as his inferior, but their relations remained cordial since his neighbour turned to him whenever in need of support. From time to time, it crossed Constantin's mind to expand south of the Foirthe fjord, but hitherto he had preferred to keep peace with the nearest southern kingdom.

Canny as ever, Constantin revealed only what he desired to Aethelflaed, and so the talk swirled on around his drooping eyelids. He did not miss anything of importance, above all they would meet *'on matters of great import'* the next morning in the same hall. The servants would have a hard time cleaning and tidying, Constantin gazed around him at the mess. His sigh expressed his weariness; he was not the first to retire, but as soon as his head touched the bolster, he fell into a deep refreshing slumber.

Sharp-witted and well rested, Constantin entered a transformed hall, restored to its utmost splendour. He approached and sat beside his nephew where he exchanged small talk.

Aethelflaed did not keep them waiting long, she rose from her seat, a regal figure, inseparable sword in its bejewelled scabbard catching the eye. Constantin admired the force of her personality, he and all the other men in the hall, hanging on her word. When it came, it shocked them all, provoking a clamorous discussion.

"Kings, lords, bishops, I have invited you here today for one reason only. I have decided to put an end to the Vikings..."

Constantin laughed aloud and was not alone in doing so. He stared at the intrepid woman who appeared unflustered by the commotion she had caused. A few minutes and the din subsided on its own, she continued, "...the scourge has troubled our people for too long. We must stamp out their pillaging and slaughtering."

The perplexity among the gathered kings, bishops, ealdormen, and aethelings at the practicality of such an enterprise, no-one seemed to find other than whisperings to an immediate neighbour. Constantin's nephew, the King of Strathclyde, rose and waited to speak. A tilt of her blonde head and he proceeded to ask, "Lady, how do you propose to do that?"

She favoured Owain with a smile warm enough to melt an icicle. Constantin, cynical, muttered under his breath, "Ach, lassie, ye'll need more than charm. Gi' us a convincing argument."

Aethelflaed went on to do so. "Half the battle is won, Sire, before we attack. To bring together the might of the north, Mierce and Wealas is enough to smite terror into the heart of the stoutest jarl. Speaking of which, I intend to strike at the very heartland of the Viking possessions here in Angle territory. Take Deoraby, and the other boroughs will fall. My brother Edward has control of the south. His mighty fortresses stood firm against every Viking assault. Swear to join me in this and you have my word, the end of the bane that afflicts our lands will be nigh."

Constantin, ignoring the raised voices and debate around him, leant over to Owain. "She's right, you know. If we all band together, the Norsemen will be helpless."

"But to sustain her against Deoraby would mean leaving our territories undefended and marching for weeks to arrive here."

"Undefended, you say? Who's to attack? Aethelflaed destroyed the Viking fleet, or rather, he did." Constantin pointed out Ecgwulf, sitting next to the Lady. "The Norsemen are in no state to cross the Irish Sea in any number. Not this year."

As they discussed this, the same arguments swirled around them from the men of Wealas and Northanhymbre. The first to support Aethelflaed's scheme, and Constantin saw it as natural, were the ealdormen of Mierce who promised warriors and money. They were the most vulnerable to the Vikings. The more he thought about the proposal, the more it appealed to him. The assurance of help from the south should the sons of Imair seek revenge on him drove him to accept.

"Lady Aethelflaed," he said when he caught her attention, "count on the Scottas for the assault on Deoraby. With that burh in your hands, the Danes will be crippled and the approach north more difficult for the Vikings in the future. We shall need until the next moon to march down to Deoraby."

Aethelflaed nodded and thanked him. She needed the agreement of the other kings, but this she regarded as the most important breakthrough. Sure enough, the other British kings followed his example, for Constantin was the senior and most highly considered among them.

The moot concluded by the acceptance of, marking and sealing of a document.

Five weeks later, in the month of July, Constantin and Owain joined their forces to those of the Miercians, Bernicians, and the men of Powys, Gwent, and Dyfed. The Danish chieftain, ruler of Deoraby, together with the Danes of Ledecestre and Northantone was engaged in raiding into Mierce. Aethelflaed, well informed of their movements, took advantage of the weakened burh and led the assault. The Viking defenders met the coalition force outside the walls of the town but let themselves be encircled and trapped. Slaughter on a grand scale ensued, giving the allied army an overwhelming victory. After initial resistance at the gate with minor losses to the attacking host, the besiegers battered the obstacle down and entered the settlement. Danes are stalwart fighters; but outnumbered to this extent, they lay down their arms and submitted to Aethelflaed. She prevented the victors from plundering the town in return for a promise of silver and gold to be raised in taxes on the conquered Danes.

Constantin travelled north to go home richer by the most direct route, through hostile country, fortified by the columns of

Bernicians and the men of Strathclyde. The trouble-free journey meant he slept in his own bed before the end of August. The expedition south could be considered a success, and the strength of the British when united proved formidable. It came as no surprise to him when he received news of the submission of Ledecestre and, more importantly, of Eoforwic to Aethelflaed. Ragnall, the Norseman, had taken the town and set his avid eyes on Ealdred's lands in Bernicia. That he would never accept, the Vikings on his doorstep. With the alliance holding firm, Ragnall had no choice but to make peace with the powerful Miercians. Lady Aethelflaed had won the esteem of Constantin, who was prepared to honour his agreement whenever called upon to do so. Likewise, one false move from Ragnall and he would call on the Miercians.

It came as a hammer blow to the King of the Scottas to learn of the unexpected death of Aethelflaed in June of 918. He would wait for events to unfold before deciding how to react.

918 AD

THE WINTER PASSED WITH ITS USUAL HARDSHIPS, BUT THE renewed hope of rebirth occasioned by the fresh shoots of spring became dashed on the twelfth day of June. All the work Aethelflaed had put into settling the kingdom came to an end with her sudden, unexpected death. Mine was by no means the only heart in Mierce broken by her passing.

The Miercian Witan gathered in haste to decide that the body of Aethelflaed should be transported to Glevcaestre for burial beside the remains of her husband. They also determined, against my advice, her daughter, Aelfwyn, should be her successor. I managed to silence Athelstan, who knew he ought to be King of Mierce according to the will of his father and grandfather. To be sure, I recognised the peril this would place him in.

The time was not ripe for such a move. I won his obedience with a promise that I would strive to ensure his dream came true. For once, the impatient youth heeded his uncle's advice to cloak his ambition. Understandably, the Witan trusted Aethelflaed and her daughter, so for less than a year, we placed our swords at the service of a new Lady, Aelfwyn. Fine a woman as she was, she could never reach the heights of her mother. Upright and merciful, ay, but shrewd she was not.

---

919 AD

HER ELEVATION DID NOT MEET WITH THE APPROVAL OF the overlord of Mierce, my erstwhile wife-brother, King Edward. Three weeks before Christ's Mass 919, Aelfwyn's uncle, King Edward, marched into town, fresh from destroying the Danish stronghold at Snotingaham, to deprive his niece of her authority before taking her back to Wessex. Full of resentment, the Mercians sullenly recognised Edward as their King while she joined a nunnery, there to live out her life. The three Welsh kings still residing in Tame Weorth – Hywel, Clydog, and Idwal – also bent the knee to Edward.

Once again, Edward disappointed. Why did he not make Athelstan King of Mierce immediately? By not doing so, he put the young man in mortal danger. In Mierce, he came under pressure to lead a revolt to liberate the 'kingdom,' which he shrewdly fended off, whereas in West Seax, he was seen as a potential rebel and usurper. But I can vouch for his unwavering loyalty to his father.

It should be remembered that not all of the West Seax nobility accepted Edward as king. Among those who did were the family of his second wife, Aelflaed. They, we had to bear in mind, would pretend succession to Edward for her firstborn. It would be argued that Aelfweard, son to a reigning king, differently from Athelstan – since Edward was aetheling when he was born – had a prior claim to the throne. I know for sure that they were spreading falsities about Ecgwynn being nothing more than a pretty, low-born concubine. I'd have ripped the filthy tongues from their mouths had I heard them myself. I knew these things but had protected Athelstan from such viper venom.

There was even a tale circulating that Athelstan's mother was a shepherd's daughter who dreamt an omen in which her belly shone with the brightness of the moon. The girl was later taken into a family who served the royal house whereupon she came to the lustful attention of the aetheling Edward, who begged to sleep with her. The birth of Athelstan made the dream come true. Such was the idiocy that was implanted in the minds of the credulous by those wishing to defame my nephew.

The maturing of Athelstan into a fearsome warrior and the deaths of Aethelred and Aethelflaed now brought matters to a head. Not content that he was far away in Mierce, afraid of his strong character, these wicked nobles concocted an evil plot. The first alert came from a spy who had been infiltrated into the West Seax court by Aethelflaed.

It is also possible that Edward tired of these rumblings at his court or that he had a longer-term vision he did not share with me or Athelstan. Whatever the case, he set aside Aelflaed, who had borne him two sons and six daughters, and married

Eadgifu, declaring her 'Lady of West Seaxa.' He did this most likely to obtain her lands, although her being young and comely might have played a part. This decision strengthened the position of Athelstan politically but placed him in greater peril than before.

15

TAME WEORTH, JUNE 918 AD

My poor, darling Aethelflaed, why did you leave me so soon? The last few days have drained me. I do not wish to speak with anyone, I pick at my food and find no ease in sleep. My heart is broken.

I wander wraithlike from my quarters to the chapel where her mortal remains lie. Time passes with me on my knees beside the rough wooden coffin containing her lovely body. It is the temporary resting place of my love. Thence she will be taken to the cathedral in Glevcaestre where a more dignified sepulchre awaits her next to her husband's.

I shall accompany the procession there, and *Breath Stealer* will keep robbers at bay. There are curs who will go to any lengths to defile the tombs of the mighty. I know for sure this coffin contains Aethelflaed's jewels and her sword. I cannot imagine her in any life without these belongings, above all the weapon.

GLEVCAESTRE, JUNE 918 AD

THE JOURNEY TO GLEVCAESTRE BECAME A REGIONAL event. We left Tame Weorth's streets packed with wet-eyed mourners. Aethelflaed was so loved in the town, the people wanted to cling to her. God only knows, how much I did. The defensive walls behind us, we proceeded at a slow pace, the four restive black horses pulling the covered wagon, restrained by the driver. The banner of Mierce unfurled and fluttered in the breeze ahead of us while, next to the carriage, the emblem of her origins, the dragon of the West Seax, rippled. I gazed behind me and counted two-score armed men, woe betide any robbers set on attacking this cortège. They made up a small army of volunteers, for the most part, grim-faced men who had fought with her against the Danes. Even in death, my Aethelflaed inspired them. It was true of the countless folk on the road to Glevcaestre who turned out to clap and bless her soul on its journey. The same applied to the crowd that welcomed her into the town whose defences she had fortified.

My head spun from hunger and weariness, and I swayed in my saddle. I have little memory of the ride except for the drawn, pallid faces of the people staring in anguish at our measured passing. It came as a relief to enter the cool nave of the cathedral. My legs buckled under the weight of the coffin, and for a shameful moment, I staggered. What a figure the *Dane-slayer* would have cut had the worst occurred! As it happened, I regained my balance and my strength so that, with my three companions bearing the pall-draped box, we reached Aethelflaed's resting place.

The stone sepulchre, a simple monument, bore nothing more than a rectangular slab with a cross carved into the top. On the side of the sarcophagus, the letters of her name swum before my unfocused, tear-filled eyes. Below the name I managed to read the legend, 'Lady of the Miercians.' She was my lady as much as she had been that of Aethelred who had lain cold in the monument to the right these past seven years. To the world, I was nobody but a friend to Aethelflaed, so discreetly had we conducted our relationship whereas she would rest forever, a wife beside her husband. Grief-stricken, inconsolable, I helped place the wooden coffin on the pavement. We struggled to remove the heavy stone cover of the sepulchre by sliding it backwards with a scraping sound that echoed in the silence of the religious sanctuary.

It needed all my courage and self-control to open the lid of the oak box wherein she lay. Serene, dressed in her finest silk, Aethelflaed, in this dim light, looked as if she were sleeping. I gasped at the sight of her one last time and roughly pushed back a thegn who reached to lift her.

"Stand back! All of you!" I hissed with a venom that must have surprised my companions. "This is my duty."

No-one dared to gainsay me. Gently, I slid my hands under her precious waist and back and lifted her clear of the wooden container. One last time, I held her in my arms, and I turned to carry her to the sepulchre. With my back to the others, I bowed my head to kiss the wheat-coloured tresses falling about her face. With all the delicacy I possessed, I laid my love inside the smooth stone receptacle. This time I bent to kiss her brow and cared not who saw.

"Farewell, Lady," the two words came so choked I doubted the others would understand. One passed me her inseparable sword, and I placed it along her left flank. Another came with handfuls of gems; like Aethelflaed, they seemed lifeless in this dimness. My futile thought was they might sparkle in Paradise on her awakening. We placed them with care inside the sarcophagus before struggling to replace the heavy lid. It took our combined strength to heave it into position. The task completed, we knelt and bade a final farewell to the Lady of the Miercians. At least, the others did. Empty of sensation and wounded inside, I was destined to return every day for the foreseeable future.

Good sense regained, time ground by, and I resumed eating, although sleep eluded me. My strength returned, which was vital as events transpired. I spent long hours praying or, rather, thinking of Aethelflaed beside her monument. Such was my state of mind in those days, I could not bear to leave her.

On the fifth day, it must have been eventide, I cannot be sure for I lost my sense of the passing time inside the dim recesses of the cathedral. Whatever time it was, I rose, and my head spun from weariness. Feeling unwell, I sought another person, but the building appeared to be empty. Alone, I staggered away from Aethelflaed's tomb and reached a smooth stone column. Clinging to it for support, I slid down to the floor, where I turned to rest my back against it and, weary, I fell into a deep sleep.

The sound of scraping awoke me, it resounded as loud as men battering on their shields before a battle in the silent confines of the cathedral. What was happening? I could see the feeble light of a candle over by Aethelflaed's tomb.

By the faint flickering near the sepulchre, I could make out the dark forms of men bending over the sarcophagus. Shaking off my sluggish drowsiness, I understood: tomb raiders! No light filtered into the cathedral. They must have come at dead of night.

"There're jewels in here and a sword, ma!" an excited voice proclaimed.

A woman's voice replied, "Never mind them things! Remember what I want. Cut me some hair and prise off a couple of toenails."

At these words, I leapt to my feet enraged, drawing *Breath Stealer*. "I'll see you in Hell first!" I shouted.

The woman screamed, and to madden me further, one of the rogues grabbed Aethelflaed's sword and drew it from its jewelled scabbard.

"Put back the weapon if you care for your life," I said, taking two steps toward the villains. The little light picked out the glint of knives. "Replace it if you wish to live. Do you not know me? Ealdorman Ecgwulf, or to you, *the Dane-slayer*. Do it! Or I'll take your head off your shoulders."

The fool would not be warned. In his greed, with the prize almost in his hands, he thrust caution aside and rushed at me wielding the blade like a banner above his head. I was faced with an inexpert loon and his fellow defilers armed with knives, but my greatest enemy at that moment was the darkness. To sustain me was my simmering fury at what they were about. I deflected the pathetic blow the scoundrel aimed at me, surprised at the sparks caused by the clash of steel. In daylight, I had never seen sparks from a blade, except from a grindstone. In the dark, rather than glimpse the other assailant, I heard the sound of his footstep and the rustle of his garments. With a quick flick of my wrist, *Breath Stealer* struck. The scream and clatter of a knife on the pavement advised me one of the curs was out of the action.

There was no time to gloat, from the other side, an unseen figure grabbed my free arm.

"Strike now!" he ordered. "Aaargh!"

Pain cut off his words as my hilt, brought down with all my might, smashed into his restraining hand. I kicked out at him and at the same time parried the flashing blade of Aethelflaed's sword. Had my opponent been an expert swordsman, I would be a dead man. As it was, *Breath Stealer* sped with an underhand thrust, and the thump of a body falling to the floor meant

8

another was out of the reckoning. I had no clue as to the effectiveness of the blow. The villain was not deceased. That much I knew from his groaning.

I needed to take the initiative.

"Woman!" I cried. "Where are you?"

"Over here, Lord!"

"Then get you a candle and tend to this wretch." I did not care a whit for the cur, but I needed light. To my grim satisfaction, the woman approached with a flickering flame. It was enough to alert me to another attack. Profiting from the illumination, a knifeman leapt my way, dagger raised. It was his last act on this Earth. Swift as a striking adder, I buried my blade in his heart, and he crashed backwards lifeless against Aethelred's tomb.

By the candlelight, I saw one man leant against a column holding his slashed arm, trying to stem the flow of blood. The swordsman, on the floor, clutched his side where a large wet patch soaked into his tunic. The woman, a dark-haired beldam, fussed over the wounded man on the pavement.

From what I could gather from the garbled exchanges, their uncouth speech distorted by the echoes in the vast space, these two were widowed mother and son.

I turned to the third man.

"You will make no attempt to flee else I will send you to Hell to join him." I jerked my head towards the corpse slumped against the sepulchre.

"As you say, Lord!"

"We will await daylight and the arrival of a priest."

I went over to Aethelflaed's sword, picked it up, reunited it with its scabbard, sheathed it, and replaced it in the tomb. This I managed, aided by the poor light cast by a guttering candle left burning on the edge of the sepulchre. I could not bear to let my gaze linger upon Aethelflaed in that ghastly light. I murmured, "I'm sorry my love," and hastened away.

The early morning brought a priest and a group of nuns for a service. They stared in horror at the bloody, sacrilegious scene but were more horrified at my explanation of the thwarted defilement.

"I cannot replace the lid on her tomb. It took four men to heave it into position days ago."

"Worry not, Lord Ecgwulf, the sisters will put it back," an elderly nun told me.

I doubted the nuns would have the strength, but eight of them struggled to heft and slide the stone cover until it settled back into position.

The priest admonished the widow. At my approach, he looked up.

"I know these wretches," he said. "They are mother and son and live down by the river. They are in dispute over land in another part of Mierce near a village called Aegelswurth."

"What has this to do with what happened here this night?"

"Sadly, everything. The woman admits to practising dark arts. She insists she did not seek riches from the tomb but hair and other from the dead Lady as ingredients for her fiendish work. It is an abomination! *The Bible*, in 'Exodus,' tells us witches are not to be allowed to live. She says she is casting spells against the rival claimant, a certain Aelsie."

The Abbess, the elderly nun, organised the sisters, for there was much needed doing.

"You four, carry the body into the vestry for the moment. Sister, run to fetch the infirmarian. The wounded have lost much blood." She turned to the priest with an exasperated expression. "What about this sinful creature?" She meant the witch.

"Send one of your sisters to bring the Scir Reeve. He will know what is to be done in the King's name."

The Abbess nodded and gave directions to another nun who hastened to do her bidding.

"Lord Ecgwulf, will you stand guard over these wretches until the Reeve comes? For I must prepare the church for service." To purify the holy building, he returned chanting prayers and swinging a censer billowing a sickly-sweet incense that caught in my throat and made me cough and sneeze.

The nuns all knew what to do and filed to the front of the cathedral where they began to sing a lovely psalm. I followed the service very little because my eyes were on the would-be tomb raiders. Now there was daylight inside the cathedral, I studied my night-time assailants. The son of the witch lay deathly pale through loss of blood, but I was convinced the wound I had inflicted was not mortal. My experienced eye suggested the blade had missed vital organs. I had not struck to kill, fighting in the dark, blind for practical purposes. His widowed mother, seeing me considering them, glared at me, and her look was one of pure evil. I believe I would have thought this not knowing, as I did, she was a servant of the devil.

It came as a relief when the Scir Reeve arrived with a group of sturdy men. They seized the wounded man and the woman.

The Reeve, a stocky fellow, whose long beard was tied to a point with a leather thong, approached me. He bowed. "Lord Ecgwulf, what a happy chance you were in the building this night, otherwise these villains would have defiled the Lady's tomb. Lord, I was under your command when we destroyed the Danish fleet."

I clasped the Reeve's hand. "What happens to these now?"

"I must gather evidence, Lord, then they will be tried by the King's court. Pray tell me what occurred here this night?"

My account finished, the Reeve inspected the body in the vestry and ordered it removed.

"You may be called to provide testimony at the trial, Lord Ecgwulf." These were his last words before leading his prisoners away.

The service continued at the front of the cathedral, but I did not remain until its end. When the infirmarian arranged for the wounded man to be carried to the abbey, I also left but not before scraping candle wax from Aethelflaed's sepulchre with a blade.

"Farewell, my love. I shall stay away from this place for a while, but fear not, for I carry you in my heart wherever I go."

Strange to relate, that same evening, Aethelflaed was foremost of my thoughts but in a different way from my recent self-torment. Invited to a feast to honour her memory organised by the grateful townsfolk, I found a place at the high table of a fine hall. There, many of us had a pleasant surprise when an eminent local ealdorman rose from his seat and began a eulogy of the life of Aethelflaed. He dwelt on her many achievements and her part in transforming Glevcaestre into an important market town with its own fairs. Finished, to our delight, he called on a scop to regale us with a song of her life. This is what he sang to the accompaniment of his lyre:

Heroic Aethelflaed! Great in martial fame,
A man in valour, woman though in name:
Thee warlike hosts, thee, nature too obeyed,
Conqueror o'er both, though born by sex a maid.
Changed be thy name, such honour triumphs bring.
A queen by title, but in deeds a king.
Heroes before the Mercian heroine quailed:
Caesar himself to win such glory failed.

When the last note died away, I leapt to my feet and led the clapping and cheering. If ever a song captured the essence of a person, this was it. I slipped a gold band off my arm and took it to the scop as a reward for his effort. For once, I retired to bed with spirits raised and fell into a deep sleep, rising late and only at that hour because of a hammering at my door.

There stood the Scir Reeve, come to inform me of his investigation.

"Lord Ecgwulf, King Edward will come to Glevcaestre to hold court on the last day of the month. I must complete my inquiries by then, but with what we found at the witch's house, I think there is little else for me to do."

"What? Tell me!"

"The people living around her are afraid when she looks at them. They say she casts the *evil eye*—"

"I'll say she does," I interrupted. "She did it to me in the cathedral – if looks could kill..."

"They say that she causes animals and people to miscarry with but a glance. But you know how folk will blather on, Lord. Anyhow, the house, now it's a different matter. She has dead crows hanging from the doorframe to start with, and we know the crow feeds on carrion, a bird worshipped by pagans. We found these." He dug into a bag and pulled out six sheep's ankle bones each inscribed with a rune. I grew up with a fear of evil magicians, and at the sight of these objects, I recoiled.

Seeing my reaction, the Reeve sighed, "Ay, for divination. 'T is the devil's work she does right enough. I broke open a closet and inside was this!" With a flourish he pulled forth a small doll, a figure of a man with red hair, beard, and his features carefully worked in clay. But what made me gasp were the nails driven into the body of the figurine. Five nails. "See, do you know who this is, Lord?"

I confessed I did not.

JOHN BROUGHTON

"It's the perfect likeness of Aelsie, the man in a dispute with them over land in the east of the kingdom. They were due to take the question to the King for settlement at the end of the month. It looks like the witch couldn't wait for the King's judgement. The matter's assumed a different hue now; for according to Wulfstan, the witch uttered a curse and laid it on his father. Since then, he's taken to his sick bed. Now there's the fact of the defiling of the Lady's tomb and she being the King's sister and all. King Edward might not take the matter too kindly."

The Reeve left me to ponder his news. I dwelt on my life too. I'm not what you might call a religious person, but I know I must answer to God. Evil exists in this world, and I had seen it at work in the form of the witch. I shuddered and mused about life. Aethelflaed's had been taken without warning. Might it happen to me? Would I be prepared? I have not led an evil life, but I often broke the fifth Commandment, "Thou shalt not kill." I am a warrior, and that is what warriors do. I groaned and sat at the table with my head in my hands.

That is when I took an important decision. I am a wealthy man. My estates provide me with more than enough money. To this income is added my share of the spoils of victory. My coffers are in rude health. I shall make arrangements to endow a plot of my lands in Kent to the Church. I will have built a church out of my fortune, and each week a mass will be sung to my soul. After this business in Glevcaestre is over, I shall travel to Kent and see to it.

On the last-but-one day of the month, King Edward arrived and sent for me to ride to the Royal Palace outside the town. There, in the hall, my erstwhile wife-brother embraced me. He wasted no time before questioning me about the events in the cathedral. His sharp mind did not miss the fact I had been inside after dark.

"You must have loved my sister right well to spend so much time at her tomb."

"I loved her, it's true," I said with conviction, and he raised an eyebrow. I would not be led on to betray my past, "but Sire, it's as I say, I was weary and fell asleep."

From there, I recounted the events of that night as I remembered them.

Edward looked shocked.

"My father's laws are clear," he quoted: "'...*women who are wont to receive enchanters, magicians, and witches, do not allow them to live.*' What then of the enchanters, magicians, and witches themselves? Is their case not worse yet?"

I nodded. "The Scir Reeve will produce damning evidence of this witch's activities.

"We shall hear the case against her in this hall on the morrow. What news of Athelstan of Mierce? Come tell me all over a beaker of mead."

In the morning, the hall was crowded. The king's court was as ever, open to those subjects who wished to attend. This case, involving a witch and also the defilement of the tomb of their heroine, captured the local imagination. My attention was drawn to the arrival of a shaky, red-bearded man leaning on the arm of a sturdy ceorl. this fellow was the same as the effigy the Reeve had shown me days before. They must be Aelsie and Wulfstan. this was confirmed when the Reeve's men forced a way through the gathering for them to approach the King. They halted near the glaring widow.

Edward called my name, and the Reeve's men led me to the front of the hall where the King sat flanked by armed warriors. He wore his crown for the occasion, and I was struck by what a regal figure he cut.

"Lord Ecgwulf, I call upon you to relate the events that

took place on the twentieth night of this month in the cathedral of Glevcaestre."

I began what, by now, was an oft-repeated tale and concluded it without hesitation, although it had been interrupted more than once by cries of outrage from the assembled folk.

"Do you swear in God's name that what you have said is the whole truth?"

"I do, Sire."

"I call upon the Scir Reeve. Let us hear your evidence, man."

The Reeve related what he had told me in my home. When he produced the nailed doll, I feared the witch would be torn limb from limb there and then, such was the outcry. His tale ended, the Reeve had to swear an oath. That done, the King called a priest.

"Father, what does the Church say about witchcraft?"

"The Church condemns all forms of divination, Sire, all worship of stones, wells, and trees. In particular, the practice of killing by witchcraft and the pricking of an image is loathsome before God. *The Bible* is clear both in the Old and the New Testaments. The Book of 'Revelations' says: But the cowardly, the unbelieving, the vile, the murderers, the sexually immoral, those who dabble in magic arts, the idolaters, and all liars – will be consigned to the fiery lake of burning sulphur. This is the second death." The first death, Sire, is ordained here by Man.

"This is in accordance with King Alfred's laws. I condemn this woman to death by drowning. The disputed lands now pass to the Crown and, I, Edward, King by the grace of God, consign them to Aelsie and his heirs in perpetuity."

The wild cheering in the room replaced the complete silence of the crowd who had hung on every word up to that point. The Reeve grabbed a staff from one of his men and beat it on the floor, for the King had not finished.

When silence was restored, the King declared, "We will not tolerate defilement of tombs in our realm. Perpetrators will be dealt a severe punishment. Let it be known. The first to feel our wrath will be those wounded in the cathedral by Lord Ecgwulf. Now," Edward pointed at the witch, "take this vile creature to the river and fulfil our sentence."

I admit I followed the crowd to the Saefern for I feared that if I did not see her die, she would return at night to haunt my dreams. I had been aware of her hateful eyes upon me when I delivered my testimony against her but had deliberately averted mine to avoid meeting her glare.

I forced a way to the front of the crowd when we reached the river bank. Most people moved aside grudgingly when they realised who I was. Two of the Reeve's burly men clung on each arm of the kicking, spitting witch. The priest stood in front of her, begging her to repent before dying. When he made the sign of the cross, her visage contorted, and she spat in the face of the poor fellow.

"Enough!" roared the Reeve. "Proceed."

I watched them haul the witch down the bank and wade into the water until both men, much taller than her, stood up to their necks in the river. There was no trace of the witch except for a series of bubbles breaking the surface and the water around the motionless men agitated by the thrashing crone. They stood there for many minutes in the now still water. There was no trace of bubbles. At last, the Reeve called, "Fetch her out!"

At his command, the two giants hauled the limp, lifeless body up the bank. Unable to keep their grip underfoot, they slithered backwards, but two more of their companions offered willing hands to drag them on to the dry ground. The Reeve raised his voice, "Let this be a lesson to us all. May this be the end awaiting anyone who has truck with Satan and his works. Bury the witch here in unconsecrated ground."

The time had come for me to turn my back on Glevcaestre and on the dead. Time to dedicate myself to the living. Should I go to Kent or check on Athelstan in Tame Weorth? I decided on the latter course of action and what a blessing I did!

16

TAME WEORTH, 920 AD

The information gatherer rode to Tame Weorth in the spring to tell me he had overheard a scheme to blind Athelstan. Without his sight, any claim to kingship he might nurture would have no substance. In my anger at this referral, I nigh on seized the poor messenger, only restraining myself with difficulty.

"Who did you overhear," I hissed, my teeth so clenched the words issued scarcely intelligible.

"One who goes by the name of Alfred."

"An insult to the name of our King of beloved memory."

"Ay, Lord, but one of a noble family," and he whispered their tribal name so no other should hear.

There is truth in the old saying *'a man forewarned is a man forearmed,'* or something of that ilk.

When a band from West Seax came to Tame Weorth and used that appellation, I was on my guard and insisted on sleeping in a room next to Athelstan's bedchamber. By day, I never let up my watch over my nephew, following him everywhere like a faithful hound. After three uneventful days, I wondered whether the attempt was a but a figment of the messenger's imaginings. On the third night, I realised it was not.

I am a light sleeper, and an unusual sound awoke me. Seizing *Breath Stealer*, I arose and walked to the door of my room, where I strained to listen for anything untoward. It came in the form of voices from Athelstan's bedchamber. I relaxed. The ram must have a ewe to tup! Trust him!

I thank the stars I did not have faith in my conjecturing. What alerted me was another muffled voice such as comes from a man with a hand clapped over his mouth.

Without further thought, I burst into the chamber and, benefitting from surprise, was in time to save Athelstan's sight. At a glance, I saw two varlets pinning my nephew's arms and a rogue heating the blade of a sword to cherry red in the fire. They had gagged Athelstan with the sort of silk scarf worn by a lady – likely found to hand in his bedchamber. In an instant, I was on them in a fury, my memory transported to another night when Athelstan was a babe. I saved him then and I rescued him now despite my near naked state. The three men, warriors all, proved no match for the enraged *Dane-slayer!* As the first of the two pinning Athelstan toppled dead at his feet, my nephew broke free from the other and made for his sword hanging from the bedhead. Doubtful as to what action, who to attack, the second hesitated. This is most unwise in the presence of *Breath Stealer,* not that the dog had time to reflect on his error before my sharp blade ended his wretched life.

The third man, their leader the scoundrel, advanced upon me with an ardent blade destined to the eyes of Athelstan. The thought induced a murderous calm in me – a state much more dangerous than blind fury. My one intention was to turn the tables on the uninvited guest. Imagine my anger when Athelstan thrust me aside with, "This one is mine, Uncle!"

I did not worry in the least Athelstan could better him, so I stood back and watched in fascination at the strident flashing blades clashing in the confined and dimly-lit chamber. How I blessed Osbald, as I too had adopted his trick of training at twilight. It paid off now as Athelstan sent his adversary's sword clattering to the stone-paved floor. I was on it in a trice whilst the tip of Athelstan's weapon pressed against the throat of the would-be slayer. My first thought was to thrust the blade back into the fire to make it glow once more.

"Shall I slay the cur, Uncle?"

"Stay! We have business with him," I said in more of a growl than a voice.

Withdrawing the red-hot sword from the fire, I moved on the coward and enjoyed the quaking of his legs and the sweat on his brow,

"Now," I said to the man who never shifted his eyes from the heated blade, "tell it true or you will taste this metal. Who sent you?"

Athelstan lowered his weapon from the fellow's gullet enough for him to speak.

"No-one."

"You lie!"

I rested the searing blade on the tip of my nephew's sword, close enough for the heat to scorch the captive's throat.

"No-one sent me, I tell it true!"

"What is your name, cur-dog?"

By now, his eyes were wild, and he screamed rather than said, "Alfred."

"Alfred of the Cynegilsing?"

"Ay."

His surprise at my knowledge made me sneer.

"And why were you heating this blade when I came in?"

No fool, he refused to reply.

"Answer me, swine-hound, or I'll give you reason not to speak."

I brought the ardent blade to his lower lip, and he screamed.

"Answer!" I cried over his scream.

"To blind him!" he blurted.

"Seize him, Athelstan, and hold him tight, a seax across his throat. Slit it if he makes a move!"

I plunged the blade back into the fire. Guessing my intention, the West Seaxa moaned and pleaded for the mercy he would not have shown Athelstan.

"Do you think I am more merciful than you, scum?" I put it to him.

"Ay, Lord," came the villain's hopeful reply.

"Would you say I am twice as merciful as you?"

"I would, lord."

"And you are right. I shall put out the one eye only."

And that is what I did. I did not enjoy the cruel deed, but my thought was to end similar attempts on Athelstan. In this way, the one-eyed varlet was a testimony to what awaited others of his clan, should they dare venture against either Athelstan or me in the future.

In my mercy, I decided to take him to the abbey, whose infirmarian might best treat his wound. I left Athelstan to dispose of the bodies. I suggested a short trip to the midden. "Take care not to be seen," I warned. "There are others from West Seax."

Saint Editha's Abbey stood close to the Royal Palace. The short distance was the fortune of the wretched Alfred, who, clutching the silk scarf to his left eye, staggered moaning and leaning on my arm to the convent gates. We were admitted by an anxious nun, who, tut-tutting and shaking her head, hurried to fetch the infirmarian. While we awaited the woman, I warned Alfred.

"Remember this, you owe me a debt of gratitude. I spared your right eye. In exchange, you will ride back to Wintancaestre as soon as you can. Take your other men with you. No further attempts are to be made on Athelstan. Harm as much as a hair on his head, and I –"

The rest was left to his imagination because the healer had joined us accompanied by a gaggle of sisters.

"Sister, this unlucky fellow has lost an eye to a searing blade and his lip is burnt. I beg you to tend to him. Please accept an offering for the upkeep of your premises." I unhooked the scoundrel's bulging purse from his belt and handed it to the grateful infirmarian.

"Take good care of your sound eye," I murmured so only he could hear me. It was meant, and no doubt taken, as a threat.

17

HETHBETHE BRIGG, 920 AD

Resentment smouldered in Mierce at Edward's treatment of Aelfwyn but also at his reorganisation of the western part of the kingdom into new scirs. The redrawn borders, running rough-shod over the older divisions of territory, caused outrage. King Edward, however, had a vision, and to fulfil his dream, he shifted his attention to the River Trente. In his grandfather's day, the Vikings had rowed downriver from a coastal anchorage and taken the populace by surprise. He was determined it should never happen again. What he had in mind for Snotingaham, he enacted elsewhere. Not even he could be everywhere at once, so he called upon his trusted men in Mierce: Athelstan and me.

"Athelstan, I want you to take charge of erecting the new fortress at Wilford. Oversee the construction of a bridge where the Leen runs into the Trente. Ecgwulf, it goes without saying that you will fight off any attempt at disturbance by the Danes. Any questions?"

"Father, I know nothing of bridge building."

"You need not worry, there is a master engineer for that.

Your task is to organise the workforce and the wherewithal to complete the building work. It is essential this is done for the safe transportation of our armies over a potentially dangerous crossing. We shall make Mierce more secure for ourselves and for our children's children."

With these words in mind, we rode to the place known as Hethbethe, and a miserable quag it proved to be. There, the master in charge of the works assured us, the river bed was suited to the construction of a bridge. He unrolled a tube of paper with a drawing of the proposed structure. The first job was to fetch logs from the vast forest nearby for the fashioning of two piers and three trestles. The latter would be settled in the deeper part of the river. I looked from the sketch to the Trente. How on earth he was going to span such a width of water, I could not imagine. The engineer must have read the doubts on my face.

"It's a fair stretch, I'll give you that, but it can be done all right. The sooner we transport the wood, the better."

Athelstan tore his eyes from the plans and became a shouting, arm-waving taskmaster. He rode out to the south of the Trente on an expedition to gather oxen, carts, and men. Within days, we had one hundred of the beasts yoked up and ready to go into the forest with thrice the number of men. They loaded the wagons with axes and saws so that, in a week, the muscular animals returned, slipping along the causeway with cartloads of tree trunks.

I became fascinated by developments because, despite having seen the drawing, I could not conceive of any edifice spanning the wide river. The ordered activity near the bank was real enough, with workers stripping bark from the trunks and beginning to saw planks.

"Lord, pray send carts to the quarry. We'll need good sandstone."

"It shall be done," I replied, knowing by now it was better not to query his requests. The price to pay for questioning was to endure a long, boring, detailed explanation.

Athelstan proved less wary. First, he asked me, "Why do you think they are making yon great box?"

The labourers were hammering together a large diamond-shaped receptacle. At a rough guess, its size must have been eight by five yards, and it contained horizontal braces to form a base frame.

"Dunno," I scratched my head, "ask him." I tossed my head towards the engineer.

Ingenuous, Athelstan, too busy to have much to do with the fellow so far, enquired.

"Yon's for a pier, Lord. I'll have it filled with sandstone rubble and sink it to the bed, see? Upright posts'll go in the four corners, well braced, and the bridge'll rest on it. There'll be another, off the opposite bank."

"Just two piers? Is that enough?"

The master laughed, "Make an engineer of you yet, Lord. Of course, two piers aren't enough! But see, the river's deeper in the middle."

"So, what will you do there."

The fellow tapped his nose with his forefinger in a gesture of smug superiority. "You just wait and see, Lord."

Had he said that to me, I might have flattened the protuberance he had touched with such self-importance, but Athelstan seemed content to swallow his curiosity and bide his time. At least the box had some sense now. It stood there like a log cabin. Within a few days, men filled both bases, there were now two, with tons of sandstone rubble for ballast and stability. I believed in the enterprise when the piers settled on the river bed leaving eight tree trunks poking out of the flowing water.

"Next stage," the master crowed, puffed up with his achievement.

After careful sounding of the depth of the centre of the watercourse from a boat, this phase turned out to be the construction of three enormous trestles. In turn, these were lowered in line with the piers, and to my amazement, the calculations were perfect. The crossbeams stood proud of the water and level with the sentinel tree trunks. Now it was clear, even to my unpractical mind, how cleverly the river would be spanned.

Tired limbs planed twenty-four trunks into beams to be rested on the piers and trestles.

"We've placed the supports close enough together so a Viking ship cannot pass through using its oars," the master announced to Athelstan. "Later, we'll make timber baulks that can be inserted in the arches just to make sure nothing passes," he said with cheery confidence.

A crane built for the purpose swung the beams into position one by one. The tenon joints settled to perfection, and men bolted them together until the two lines spanned the Trente straight as an arrow's flight.

A man could walk across the river on the beams. Before long, a challenge was thrown down to offer light relief from work. The labourers managed to cajole two of their number into a race. The winner was to receive a silver scillingas, but many more coins changed hands as betting fever took hold.

At midday, the contestants set off. The one nearest to us moved cautiously, taking small steps, his arms outstretched and level with the water. The other grinned at him and started forth at a trot. I held my breath; I'd bet on the loon! Sure enough, he slipped and ended in the water spluttering and mouthing oaths to the delight of the cheering onlookers – mainly those who had wagered against him. With an ungainly doggy paddle, he reached the bank where he was hauled out and thrust back to the beam to join the challenge again. Of course, the race was not over until one contestant stood in triumph on the opposite bank. Athelstan swore as his man wobbled and teetered. Mine had learnt his lesson, closing the gap with a sensible gait this time. I swear there may have been no more than a two-yard margin in the loss of my ten scillingas to Athelstan.

The laying of the horizontal logs to form the bridge roadway was rapid work: as quick as the felling, transport, and shaping allowed. Slower was the construction of the sturdy trellis either side, designed to prevent wagons or people sliding off into the water below. The bridge completed, little more than two moons after starting, Athelstan rode his horse across to the far bank and waved me to follow. He had ordered the transportation of more tree trunks, in vast amounts. The next stage was to build a D-shaped fortification running along the bank on the drier ground further upriver. The stronghold, demanded by King Edward, was destined to house a garrison. The idea was to hold off an enemy determined to press inland toward the rich pickings of the steadings south of the river.

Of course, this was Edward's master plan. Roads with stout bridges would facilitate the movement of the fyrd, making a conduit linking burhs to their far-flung economic and military resources, so that any incursions could be swiftly dealt with. What we had created near Snotingaham was repeated in networks throughout the south of the country. Construction work on the palisade, to which many, if not all, of our labourers were accustomed, proceeded apace.

To my relief, and that of my aching bones, Athelstan and I returned to the warmth and comfort of Tame Weorth for the mass of Saint Michael at September's close.

During our stay in the mud by the Trente, Edward did not idle away his time in the luxury of the Royal Palace in Wintan-caestre. Before we started bridge-building, he took his army to Thelwall where he built a new fortress just northeast of Aethelflaed's stronghold at Rumcofan. His aim to defend the northern border of Mierce, as usual with Edward, was sound. The Danelaw south of the Hymbre may have been almost wholly under our control, but the Norse Vikings north of the Hymbre were still a threat.

Even as we worked at the Trente, the Viking King Ragnall stormed and took Eoforwic, while Sihtric stormed Deneport, north of the Mersey. Edward, in response, led his army to Badecanwelle amid the Peaks where he raised another fortress and received the submission of the people of the north, who *chose him as father and lord.* It looked to me as if peace had been agreed, but what I did not understand was that if Ragnall's brother, Sihtric, was still issuing coins in his own name, how could Edward pretend to control the north?

The pagan Ragnall died, he who had been King of Dublin and Mann, now his brother sailed from Dublin to claim the kingdom of Northanhymbre. Although I could not know it at the time, the thorn in the side of Mierce was about to be removed forever.

In the relative peace that followed Ragnall's death, the nobles in Mierce did what people do best at times like these, they plotted upheaval. I believe it is human nature to foment discontent when offered stability and prosperity. How else can what happened in Mierce be explained?

18

TAME WEORTH, 921 AD

"Take my advice, have nothing more to do with those two
renegades!" I shouted at Athelstan, whose stupidity, in
my opinion, had slumped to a new low. I turned to stomp out of
the hall when he seized my arm to force me to stand square to
him and thrust his face into mine.

"What has Edward ever done for us? Except to betray your
sister, my mother, and break her heart? Oh, I almost forgot," he
hissed close to my ear, "he's thwarted my ambitions at every
turn, going against my grandfather's will."

I pushed him away before his anger sprayed me with his
spittle.

"How many times do I have to tell you to be patient,
Nephew? Open rebellion will bring all your hopes crashing
down like an undermined wall. Who are these 'important
ealdorman' who have wormed into your mind?"

"They hold land in the southwest of Mierce. One is
Wulfric and the other, Ealhhelm."

"Pah! Don't you know they are both of noble West Seax
families? Why would they want to put you on the throne of

134

Mierce? More likely, they want Aelfweard seated on Edward's."

"I have their loyalty."

"Would you keep a wolf as a lapdog?"

"Uncle, I thought I could count on *you!*"

"I want nothing to do with it. What they are planning is treason and not for your sake, rest assured."

"I'm tired of waiting for Edward to give me my due. What kind of father is he?"

"He is a great king, making our land a stronger and safer place. Can you not see? He wishes to make Angle-land one whole kingdom where Angles can prosper and toil in peace beside the Danes."

"It's but a dream. What world does he live in? Have you ever come across peaceful Norsemen, Uncle?"

Chafing at his nonsense, at the same time, I was worried where his ambition and impulsive nature might take him. I could think of nothing more to dissuade him except to deny him my support.

"If you insist on these treasonable plans, we must be enemies."

My words served their purpose. Athelstan looked hurt and pushed past me hopefully to calm down and clear his brain in the fresh air. Of course, I did not mean that I would fight my nephew. I loved him like the son I'd never had. But I could not go along with this folly.

King Edward was busy as ever in this year and built a fortress at the mouth of the Clwyd. It is my opinion that the King must have heard of the plot against him. I had discovered that the two ealdormen bending my nephew's thoughts were in constant contact with three Wealisc kings. The location of the new stronghold suggested to me that Edward expected trouble.

To be fair to Athelstan, I ought to point out that many influential Miercians did not agree with Edward's treatment of Aelfwyn. She had been hidden away in a nunnery, but nobody knew where. Simmering discontent about this and the new scirs in the west of Mierce developed into open opposition.

<hr />

924 AD

THE REBELS CHOSE CAESTIR AS THEIR BASE. WELL-fortified by Aethelflaed and close to the borders with Wealas, it symbolised the former might of Mierce.

"I will not join you, nor will I take up arms against my own nephew," I told Athelstan. He could not fail to see how his decision to betray his father saddened me. I am not proud of my vacillation, but what was I to do? What a choice! If I joined my King, who was marching upon Caestir with an army, I would go against Athelstan; ally with him, and I would break faith with my friend and King. As it happened, after a short siege, Edward crushed the revolt. By luck, there were few deaths, the rebels being more interested in negotiating their grievances. I am convinced that Edward withdrew to Farndune in good faith, meaning to address the problems of Mierce. Who knows whether the stress of civil war brought about his demise? Edward, my enigmatic friend and king, died there on the seventeenth day of July. His passing was as swift as it was unexpected.

It left a political conundrum. Athelstan had sided, against my advice, with the rebels, which made him less acceptable as a ruler to the West Seaxa. A strong faction based at Wintan-caestre supported the claim of Aelfweard, the eldest son of Edward by his second wife. The West Seaxa chose Aelfweard as King while the Miercians opted for Athelstan. War seemed inevitable, but less than a month after the death of Edward, in August, Aelfweard also died. This favoured the accession of his brother, Edwin.

Given that Athelstan had a legitimate claim to both thrones, I supported him without reservation. Although I did not voice my ambitions for my nephew, even to him, I decided not to rest until he became King of all England. That is, *Rex Anglorum* over a *Perfecta Saxonia* – *a united Saxonland* – was how I conceived his destiny, and true to the vision of Alfred and Edward, I would throw my heart and mind into achieving this aim. This was illusory because the West Seaxa had not opted to bend the knee to my nephew but to another.

This is when I decided to control the situation. I informed myself who were the most enthusiastic supporters of Athelstan in Mierce and, having done so, made sure to reward them amply. The wisest course of action, I believed, was to persuade Athelstan to march south with an army into West Seax and there assert his authority over 'King' Edwin. I decided the two actions should be combined into one. A thegn named Alfred, a counsellor, deserved a reward for his loyalty, so in Wintan-caestre, I granted him a charter of lands to be witnessed in the New Minster. Edwin, still young and malleable, I persuaded by charm and mature strength to sign under the signature of Athelstan. This implied he was subservient to the latter.

It soon became clear that the West Seax lords would not accept Athelstan on their throne despite him being a valiant, tested warrior. That the fomentation of discontent following the charter did not erupt into violence, I ascribe to my and Athelstan's fine reputation for military prowess. In other words, the cowards ran scared.

Athelstan kept the wheels of government grinding for almost a year; while hidden from view in Wintan-caestre, support for Edwin grew. Only by rounding up the ringleaders and keeping them far from the town was I able to arrange the coronation on the fourth day of September of 925. On that day, Athelstan became King of West Seax and Mierce. This made him effective king over all the lands south of the Hymbre. For the fulfilment of my long-term ambitions for Athelstan, I turned my attention north of that umber-coloured estuary.

It occurred to me that my unmarried niece, whose steadfast refusal to become either a nun or a wife, might serve a political purpose. Ragnall's brother, a tall, strapping Viking, now King of Northanhymbre, might be amenable to a wedding. I put the matter to Athelstan and, in spite of his natural fraternal jealousy, he consented to my plan.

JANUARY 926 AD

I RODE TO EOFORWIC WITH AETHELGYTH IN A CARRIAGE, accompanied by a suitably armed escort. She was now a maid of seven and twenty winters and fair of face, not as beautiful as my sister, her mother, but who was? My confidence that Sihtric would be taken by her comeliness proved well founded. I did not expect Aethelgyth to be so accommodating. I've never believed in instant love, but whatever affected my niece was just as effective. I noticed that her eyes passed over the Norse Viking with approval. Like many of his race, he stood tall and strong with grey-blue eyes offsetting his blond hair; unlike others, he did not bear inked symbols but becoming armlets over his bulging muscles. All told, he presented a fine figure, able to remove the main obstacle to our pact: the renowned stubbornness of my niece. The other obstacle had preoccupied me all the journey north: religion. Sihtric, a Norseman, was a pagan. He could not marry my niece unless he agreed to baptism and to renounce his gods.

I contrived to distance myself from the betrothed so they had time alone. At first, it seemed a good idea when I saw their heads close together followed by Sihtric taking Aethelgyth's hand. But strolling deeper into the Danish settlement, I thought myself not so clever as hostile glares and muttered threats came my way. What did I expect, with the epithet of *the Dane-slayer* dogging me in Eoforwic? A brute of a fellow carrying a pail slopping water drawn from a well bumped into me and drenched my leggings. It was no accident, I know, but I was here on a mission of peace and harmony.

"Watch where you're going, Saxon oaf!"

That was what he said, and I had to settle for memorising his ugly face.

My mood improved when King Sihtric returned hand in hand with my niece. They found me brooding and whittling at a stick with my short seax.

"We have an understanding, my betrothed and I," the Norse King said, causing me to leap up and seize his hand. "I will travel back to Tame Weorth with you to discuss the dowry with her brother. I will let one of your priests wet my head."

Aethelgyth's radiant smile warmed my heart, driving negative thoughts about pagan Danes out of my head. Our journey back was interrupted twice owing to the bad January weather, but at last, we rode into the capital of Mierce on the last-but-one day of the month. So, King Sihtric met with King Athelstan and made the wedding arrangements. Thus, was an attempt made to ensure peace between our two peoples. That it would come to nought remained far from our minds that happy day of feasting and song.

Of course, we held still greater celebrations when they married in the spring. Aethelgyth was not a lucky bride because King Sihtric died the following year. Before his demise, he renounced Christianity, which saddened me, for now he would roast in Hell.

———

927 AD

Upon hearing of the death of his Norse wife-brother, Athelstan marched to Eoforwic. He had not stayed long before Sihtric's brother, Gofraid, King of Dublin, sailed for Northanhymbre to contest the throne. He left the kingdom in Ireland to his sons, a poor decision...because it provoked a war between them and their cousins, Sihtric's sons. It also piqued me because I had decided now or never for Athelstan to become the King of all of the English. I'll say this for Athelstan, he is quick to agree with my best choices when it's in his interests.

When Gofraid appeared with his Vikings, we awaited and drove him out of Eoforwic. I suppose our task was made easier with Gofraid distracted by events back in Ireland. Sihtric's sons allied with Limerick and conquered Dublin. To what extent we chased and swept him away or whether he hastened to regain his kingdom depends on how much I have drunk when I tell the tale. Athelstan declared himself King of Northanhymbre and called a meeting with the other kings of Britain.

In July of that year, in the area of lakes and mounts known as Cwymry or Cumbria in the northwest of the land, Athelstan summoned a great council at Eamont Bridge. There, he brought under his rule Hywel of Dyfed, Constantin of the Scottas, Owain of Gwent, and Ealdred of Bebbanburgh.

What a gathering it was! Athelstan's plan was to demonstrate, with rich gifts and the unity of West Seax and Mierce, just how powerful he was and above all, to persuade these rulers of their common interests without spilling blood. The main drum he could beat on was each of them shared the one true faith to protect against the pagan Norsemen.

I looked around the assembled leaders to understand their attitudes. The oldest was the hoar-headed Constantin, King of the Scottas. I sensed his resentment at being summoned to the moot by a younger, albeit exquisitely-mannered monarch. Constantin had kept his people safe for nigh on thirty years and was well used to crafting alliances that shifted like quicksand. Did he really need to be bound to West Seax? I shared my nephew's desire to fix the new limits of his kingdom within the assured boundaries of a negotiated peace. But Constantin, on the face of it, had little to gain by accepting the overlordship of this young man from the far south. Even his brand of Christianity, Ionian as it was, differed from ours. If we could not agree on the dates of Easter or on monks' haircuts, what hope was there for frontiers?

I passed on to Hywel of Dyfed. He looked relaxed to me, the most amenable to Athelstan's plan. He too was older than my King but not as old as Constantin, although he had reigned for as long over his kingdom. His problem of how to patrol his long coastline facing the Viking kingdom of Dublin kept him well in line with Athelstan. The latter had taken back the Viking lands around and including what they called Jorvik. So, there were mutual interests to defend. This showed in the warm smiles Hywel directed at my Lord and King. Hywel shared another interest with Athelstan. Equally devoted in his faith, he displayed a great interest in the relics my nephew had brought on his journey. There would be no problem of persuading Hywel to put his mark on the elaborate parchment that Athelstan had prepared with its colourfully inked, curled scroll border.

What then of Ealdred of Bebbanburgh? I would not trust him had I been in Athelstan's shoes. But here, with wily eyes upon us, was not the place to voice my doubts. This young man treated his allies with suspicion, and who could blame him? His lands, compressed between Strathclyde, the lands of the Scottas, and now, Athelstan's, where once the Vikings devoured chunks of his territory, were the most vulnerable of all. It showed in his shifting eyes and shuffling feet. He had fought with Constantin against Viking raiders in the past, even spending time at Constantin's court ten years ago, but I could see theirs was an uneasy friendship. Constantin treated him with an arrogant superiority that rankled with Ealdred whose memory fed on the once great past of Northanhymbre. Instead of that glory, he found himself hemmed in surrounded by those who wished to claw back territory from him.

Hywel was the first to step forward and make his mark on the parchment. Athelstan did remarkably well not to show relief on his countenance. Only I knew how worried he was about failing to convince these proud and guileful men to do his bidding. Sure, no sooner had Hywel laid down his pen than Athelstan swept him into a warm embrace. But already, over the Wealisc man's shoulder, his eyes swept around the others to see who would next follow his example. It proved to be Ealdred, and I know he moved swiftly as a show of disrespect to Constantin. By signing before the white-haired Scot, he established himself as more important. At last, Constantin signed but not without a speech in praise of Lady Aethelflaed who, according to him, had been a devout, wise and noble warrior with whom he had come to terms over ten years before. Condescendingly, he told Athelstan that she had brought him up well to follow in her footsteps. Such was Athelstan's love of his late aunt that he failed to garner the insult implied but beamed with pleasure at the compliment that cloaked it.

So it was done. The various leaders who came with the intention of being almost equals made peace with pledges and oaths. There will be a baptism of one king's son, and others will leave a hostage behind. My nephew will come out of this moot as a man rich in wealth. They also promised not to support Gofraid or other Vikings and to suppress paganism. Later, Owain of Strathclyde joined the monarchs who bent the knee. I rejoiced, England was now *'made whole'* as in the dream of Athelstan's grandfather, King Alfred.

I oversaw the minting of new coins throughout the land and ensured they bore an abbreviation for *Rex Totius Britanniae* or 'King of the Whole of Britain.' I also counselled and prevailed on Athelstan to call the British kings to witness his charters, who appear in them as *subreguli* or under-kings to him. Instead, Athelstan appeared as *Rex Anglorum*. My own nephew had achieved what his father and grandfather had aspired to but could not attain. My wealth and power were limitless, but I did not want them for myself, only for Athelstan and love of the memory of my sister. Achievement and consolidation are two different creatures; both need taming, and the latter, I mused, might prove more savage.

19

NARRESFORD, NORDHAMPTUNESCIR, 926 AD

I wish to relate a number of episodes that occurred shortly after my nephew became King. These will illustrate what kind of man he had become. The first happened on the occasion of a folk-mote. Strictly speaking, the King was not required to attend a *folcgemot*, but as often was the case with Athelstan, he surprised everyone by overturning convention. I considered it a fatherly concern for his people and one which, as events took their course, added to the esteem and love accorded him.

On our return from a successful campaign against a Danish raiding party, the journey took us through the hundred of Narresford. There, the folk of seven settlements composing the one hundred hides of land met. According to custom, no-one attending these gatherings carried arms; the bearing of weapons being allowed only once the moot had concluded.

Unaware the King had strolled into the midst of the assembly – a pardonable lapse, since unexpected – the *gerefa*, the chief constable, addressed him in a haughty tone.

"Hey! You fellow! It is you I am talking to...how dare you enter the folk-mote with a sword at your side?"

Athelstan's colour rose, and I, who by the by, also had *Breath Stealer* at my flank, feared the worst.

It might have been better had the constable awaited a reply, however harsh, but the zealot cried, "Without a tongue, are you? Seize him!"

Breath Stealer was out in a flash before the three burly brutes directed toward my nephew could blink. Their hesitation, wise under the circumstances, allowed me to shout with relish, "Would anyone here be so bold as to lay hands on his King? Any such man must first reckon with *the Daneslayer*." Not wishing to boast in vain, it must be said the effect of my words produced the silence of a crypt. The constable's visage became as pale as an alabaster monument in an ossuary.

To give Athelstan his due, he is a quick-witted fellow, so true to form, he called, to the constable.

"Arise, *gerefa,* you cannot do your duty on your knees! Lord Ecgwulf put away your sword. It is out of place in this peaceful gathering conducted to the King's approval."

"Sire, forgive my impertinence, I had no idea..."

"Constable, pardon our intrusion. You could not know of our unannounced presence. Now, pray commence proceedings and make an exception for your King and Ealdorman Ecgwulf to bear arms this day."

What could the poor fellow say? The colour returned to his face, and he bowed at the honour the King had bestowed upon him in the implicit request for his permission.

The meeting began with the tedious business of ordinary administration, which, to be honest, bored me but not Athelstan, who followed every word with the greatest interest.

My attention was caught for the first time when the constable cleared his throat and called for any other issues.

"Well, ay," a miserable-looking fellow with lank cropped

hair in a filthy tunic glanced uneasily toward the King, "begging pardon and not wanting—"

"Get on with it, man!" the constable raged.

"It's like this: I 'ave a cousin o'er in Nassaburh an' 'e told me our Lord King Athelstan...God bless ye, Sire!...ordered to be given to the needy ev'ry month a measure o' meal, and once a year, a gammon o' bacon, or a ram worth fourpence, besides clothing. These things the *gerefa* of Nassaburh gave out ter the poor folk there but 'ere, it's anither matter. We ain't had nowt! An' there b'ain't no-one needier than my fam'ly!"

Once more, the colour drained from the constable's face.

"What do you have to say about this, Constable?" Athelstan approached the official.

"True, Sire. I neglected my duty. We received your generous edict, but I failed to execute the order, I'm ashamed to say."

If there is one thing my nephew appreciates, it is honesty. I swear it is a weakness of his. He glared at the constable.

"As well, my man," he declared in regal tone, "that you conduct an orderly moot, and it seems to me you are remiss in this sole matter. I command you to draw up a list of the needy in this hundred and to carry out my decree without delay."

"Your will shall be done, Sire."

"Have you studied the ordinance, Constable?"

"Ay, Lord."

"Then you will know failure to distribute the royal charity procures a fine of thirty scillingas, to be divided among the poor of this tything. I command you forfeit this sum."

A buzz of appreciation ran through the gathering, and many gazed upon their King with admiration, not least his uncle. This was how King Athelstan treated the lowest of his subjects.

146

WITAN-CAESTRE

I PROCEED TO THE SECOND OCCASION, AN ENTIRELY different situation. It took place in the Royal Palace at Witan-caestre and involved my nephew's dealings with affairs of state. Athelstan formed a league with Harold, King of Norway, because countless petitions arrived from traders, merchants who had lost everything to pirates, who infested the seas around our Isles. It was a matter of debate in those days whether the gales sweeping the seas or the pirates were the more perilous. Thanks to the intercession of my nephew and his ability to persuade other rulers, King Harold chased the sea robbers from his own dominions. Thence he pursued them over the seas until he caught and destroyed their ships. Thereafter, the two kings, working in harmony, drew up severe laws for the punishment of any who dared attack either English or Norwegian vessels.

King Harold held Athelstan in such high esteem that he sent his son Haco to England to be educated in the West Seax court. The young prince made such rapid progress in his studies and warlike exercises that a messenger arrived in Witan-caestre from his father, and I am pleased to report it.

"Sire, with the utmost humility, I present my King's request you accompany me, when you see fit, to the port of Hamwic. Thereupon, it will be my pleasure to consign to you a gift from King Harold."

What this gift might be bewildered those in attendance, me included. It must be something so large it could not be transported overland with ease. We speculated about it for days until Athelstan declared himself free to travel with the messenger to Hamwic. I would not have missed the occasion for the world such was my curiosity.

When we arrived at the settlement, the envoy led us straight towards the docks, where the reason for our trip became clear. At moorings bobbed the most magnificent vessel I had ever clapped eyes on. Her purple sails were furled, and she was surrounded with shields rich in gilt, while the prow was wrought out of pure gold. What a gift! All present in the royal retinue failed to find words to describe this munificence.

In Witan-caestre, Athelstan embraced Prince Haco and presented him with a costly sword, the like of which the lad might only have dreamt about. When afterwards, as king on the day of his father's death, he took the weapon to Norway and treasured it all his life. In addition, his people dubbed him King Haco the Good. I believe this due to his education at our court and copying the ways and instructions of my nephew. I explained this second episode to give insight into the wisdom and strength of Athelstan.

When Harold died, there were problems as to the succession of Haco to the throne of Norway, so Athelstan provided him with warriors and a strong fleet, enabling him to take possession of his kingdom. On the thrones of France, Bretagne, and Norway sat three kings all indebted to Athelstan for their crowns. What more can I say about the power and dignity our King had bestowed on our land?

20

EAMONT, 927 AD

Constantin was uneasy about this meeting since Athelstan mooted the idea. It would not be wise to show his inner turmoil to the others, in particular, not to the young King whose persistence had succeeded in gathering the Brittonic kings. The location of the moot troubled the King of the Scottas. Or was he overreacting? This area of rivers, lakes, and mountains lay too close to his own kingdom. Or was it courtesy on the part of Athelstan, who, with consideration, had avoided a long journey for Constantin?

Anticipating the slightest provocation, he admitted Athelstan hitherto had displayed only respect and good manners towards him. He could not evade the sensation the self-styled King of the English believed him to be old, weak, and easy to subdue. It rankled that a man who had ruled his realm for so short a time should pretend supremacy over one who had reigned with wisdom for thirty years and more.

Constantin gazed around the gathering. To arrive here, the kings from the territories of Wealas had travelled much farther than him. Was this another sign Athelstan considered him old?

Hywel was no stripling for that matter! The King paced the grass, hands clasped behind his back, irritation on the brink of betraying his feelings. The anxious eyes of Athelstan on him, following his every step, pleased Constantin. The fellow might not be as confident as he wished to appear. Good! The successful outcome of this assembly meant much to him. Let him worry!

The key to Athelstan gaining his desire, Constantin ruminated, lay in the answer to this question: *Why should I submit to an overlord?* Athelstan had brought them here without bloodshed to his table bearing the document waiting for his mark. Therein lay the essence. To which it should be considered that there was a precedent. Had not this young king's aunt created an alliance with himself and the Brittonic kings against the Danes, ten years ago? That the agreement, after serving its initial purpose, collapsed had no importance. It was the nature of allegiances. They came and went, swaying. Constantin smiled at the idea of himself as a reed bending according to the direction of the breeze. Poor Aethelflaed, what a shame she died when she did. She was a wise, self-assured, and devout woman, and brave. He felt at ease with her in a way he did not with her nephew because she and he were closer in age.

Hywel signed the accord. Constantin watched the Wealisc king straighten up and look around before his gaze settled on him. No coincidence, that. It showed Hywel's own uneasiness. If Constantin did not sign, the others would not. The reason for Hywel's submission did not escape the King of the Scottas. With a long coast to defend facing the Dublin Vikings, his kingdom was the most vulnerable and the alliance, therefore, most pressing.

Constantin again focused on why he agreed to come to the meeting. A refusal to attend would have been easy but interpreted as hostile. Athelstan proposed the moot evoking the

Christian virtue of neighbourliness – ay, *love thy neighbour*. Constantin made much of his devotion to the Church; how could he refuse to come? Wily he may be, but he was not a hypocrite. The Norsemen were pagans. A Christian alliance for defensive advantage suited all the kings gathered here, without doubt.

What other reason brought him here? Constantin frowned. There was more to this than shared Christianity. When Athelstan marched into Jorvik, Constantin's immediate reaction was peevish. The fellow had extended his kingdom from Wessex to Northanhymbre. To find such a powerful king so close to his own borders disturbed his peace of mind. But, an agreement today, with a stroke of a pen and that did not cost lives, meant a friendly king installed in Jorvik. This was a better situation than having the Vikings there waiting only for the arrival of more longships up the River Use. Would they not launch an attack into Bernicia against the weak Ealdred? With Bernicia taken, what would prevent the Vikings from pressing into his kingdom across the Foirthe fjord?

Constantin snapped out of his reverie and sauntered to the table. Reaching for the quill extended to him by Athelstan's cleric, he made his mark and heard the release of breath from Athelstan. He glanced up and caught the English King's eye. Athelstan nodded but kept his relief and satisfaction hidden, though Constantin knew those emotions consumed him. Just the time to move away from the table and the weakling Ealdred wielded the pen. It suited him far more than a sword, the Scot sneered.

The other Wealisc kings followed their lead and, in turn, ealdormen and bishops signed as witnesses. Constantin exchanged words with Hywel. The king of Dyfed, renowned for his piety, seemed more interested in the prospect of viewing the religious relics Athelstan carried on his travels. Thus,

Constantin had the opportunity to reinforce his own importance. Taking Hywel by the arm, he led him over to his baggage train and ordered the *Breccbennach* to be brought forth. Constantin, holding it on outstretched palms, presented the holy reliquary of Saint Columba. Hywel dropped to his knees in awe making the sign of the cross, his lips mouthing a silent prayer.

In an instant, Athelstan stood beside him, no doubt ensuring Hywel was not swearing an oath to Constantin. The King of the Scottas reassured him with an explanation, and the younger man, noted for his Christian devotion, joined Hywel on his knees before the reliquary. He experienced a shameful sense of superiority to have them in obeisance before him. Only, they were not, and his irritated pride needed assuaging. Restoring the holy depository to the baggage wagon, the animated discussion of the life of the Saint between the two rulers went some way to soothing him. He seized the chance to relate his favourite legend of the water monster.

"When you come as guests into my kingdom, I will take you to see the inky waters of the loch known as Ness. Therein flows the river of the same name. On a dull day, the loch is bottomless and sinister in appearance. It is said the saint subdued a ferocious water monster that killed a Pict to then attack Columba's disciple named Lugne. The Saint banished it to the depths of the River Ness." Constantin made his smile imperceptible at the effect his tale elicited on the awestruck faces of the two kings. He continued, "Folk who live near the vast stretch of the loch's waters, especially fishermen, relate sighting a monstrous head and neck emerging from the deep. Since the intervention of the Saint, no-one has seen the beast harming a soul."

"Remarkable," Athelstan murmured. "Tell me, King

Constantin, did you never think of venturing out in a boat to slay the monster?"

Constantin peered at the younger man. Was he mocking him? The expression on the countenance of the English King was awestruck, so Constantin accepted the remark.

"Like Saint George and the dragon, you mean?"

"Ay."

"I would not presume so much. Saint Columba dealt with the problem. It can be no coincidence the monster kills no more."

Athelstan glanced toward the table where servants were setting out chairs and platters.

"Come, my friends, we shall speak on this and other wondrous things over food and drink."

He led the way to the table where he took his place at the centre. Hywel did not hesitate but sat next to the Englishman. Constantin stared around and spotted the sour faces of his followers. It would not do to take a seat close to Athelstan; it would show subservience. There again, he must not sit too far away or the English king might be offended and consider Constantin an untrustworthy ally. The other kings approached. He must decide in haste. This he did, sitting next to Hywel, a place suggesting his acceptance of events but still sufficiently defiant, the precise summary of how he felt. Constantin's lip curled as Ealdred, the little toad, slid into the vacant seat at Athelstan's other side.

Hywel interrupted his brooding. "Will you tell us more about the life of Saint Columba?"

Of course! His devotion to this saint was absolute as was that of his people. So, the meal started in pleasant vein for Constantin, and aided by strong drink, he soon relaxed into a comfortable spirit of Christian neighbourliness. Knowing this to be the aim of the young English king did not matter as long as his followers did not see him as subservient to anyone. His eyes wandered time after time to the trestle table where they sat devouring meat and swilling ale in joyful abandon. Truculent and surly whenever offended, capable of battling their own shadows, when content, his subjects entered wholeheartedly into festivities. This, he assured himself, was true of the present occasion. Today did not bother him, but he was too wise and experienced to know who were the people he needed to convince about his supremacy. They would emerge, on his return home, like viscid and vile creatures from under a stone.

In the days and weeks following his encounter with the kings, he reasserted his authority. His sons, above all the eldest, cast covetous eyes on his throne as did the viper-like Malcolm. Constantin feared his cousin, Máel Coluim mac Domnaill, to honour him with his rightful name in the Pictish language, would stop at nothing to claim kingship. He did not dislike the man and reckoned him capable but found the verbal thrusts and counter-thrusts wearisome at his age. Yet, the experience and wisdom he vaunted kept his throne stable for the moment.

The first tremor after the moot at Eamont came with the arrival at Constantin's court of a messenger from Athelstan. Ealdred soon scuttled across the border from Bebbanburgh alarmed by the same communication. Whenever he considered himself challenged, Ealdred sought his neighbour's advice.

The new year brought a summons from Athelstan to his Witan. Constantin would not be called like an obedient hound by anyone, so when the message arrived, he did not deign to reply. Ealdred, give him his due, did not wish to be summoned, either. His position with Athelstan on his border required a strong character, which Ealdred did not possess. That he came whimpering to Constantin pleased the King of the Scottas. It suggested, in a straight choice, Ealdred would choose him over Athelstan.

"I most certainly will not go," he told Ealdred, "and you as King of Bernicia," flattering the man, "should not, either."

Ealdred vacillated. His weakness irritated Constantin. "You say Athelstan is unreasonable to make this demand, yet you hesitate out of fear. Be strong, refuse and be done with it. You can count on my support." Constantin fanned the flames of Ealdred's resentment. It meant the alliance so painstakingly constructed by Athelstan had crumbled within a year, but what did he care? He had a kingdom to keep stable and Máel Coluim to repel. What a chance for him to demonstrate Constantin was no longer worthy to rule if he journeyed south and abandoned his realm at a snap of Athelstan's fingers. No, he would not give him that opportunity.

Whatever decision he took, however, whichever way he glowered, Constantin could see only storm clouds gathering on the horizon.

21

WINTAN-CAESTRE, 933 AD

I n the southwest of our kingdom, local fishers say: *"the fish rots from the head."* When ruling, it means you should look close to the throne for the first signs of revolt. Edwin had left his childhood well behind and grown into a strapping fellow. With his increased strength grew a desire to remove the King from a position certain serpentine voices continued to hiss was his birthright.

For all their machinations, our spies informed us of the threatened uprising so that I prepared for the day with the utmost care. The first counter-measure was to arrest Edwin and bring him before his half-brother, Athelstan. I accused him of plotting against his King, which the pale-faced villain denied vehemently.

I had him marched to the Old Minster to deny it under oath over the remains of Saint Birinus, who converted the West Seaxa and founded the church in Wintan-caestre. Especially revered in these parts, the saint would not take kindly, I figured, to a blatant lie. A similar thought must have afflicted Edwin, judging by his haunted expression. Somehow, he found the nerve to proceed. I decided on the instant he would pay in this world for his sin.

For the present, I had his every movement watched, so when armed men broke into the King's Hall, we met them in force. Two-score bodies lay on the blood-soaked rushes of which ten were those of our men. In the heat of combat, I was grateful my men heeded my shrill cries to take alive the last enemy standing.

Our threats of horrific torture failed to loosen the wretch's tongue. I wanted his confession that Edwin had sent the rebels. We extracted it from the miserable fellow in the end, but not without the persuasion of red-hot iron. I'll never understand why a simple man should sell his life for another richer and more powerful. I admired his pluck and regretted being unable to save him.

The heads of his comrades, and his, we impaled on stakes displayed on the walls of the town to deter other plots against Athelstan. Carrion crows showed their infinite raucous appreciation. Edwin and other plotters fled toward the coast on horses, and the King begged me to ensure their exile. More than willing to comply, I headed off in pursuit, but my idea of banishment for Edwin involved leaving this world.

We chased them into the port of Hamwic, and having taken the precaution of bringing with me my most expert spy, I set him loose. This is how we discovered where they were staying and from whom they intended to hire a boat as soon as the adverse weather improved to allow for sailing to Frankia. I decided to speak with the captain myself. My trusted informant led me into the malodorous port where the stench of spoil mingled with that of fish entrails forced me to cover my nose.

The weather-beaten face of the seaman scanned mine with suspicion bordering on insolence. I spoke with authority, "Heed me well, fellow. With this beauty," I tapped the hilt of

Breath Stealer, "I have slain more Danes than times your ship's crossed to Frankia. This blade is in the service of our rightful King Athelstan, God bless him, and is sworn foe to any who work against him." I drew *Breath Stealer* with quiet deliberation and let the sailor scan it as he had my countenance. Easy to see my threat needed taking no further, I sheathed my sword and patted the fellow on his back. "Now, to business, how much has the rebel promised you to ferry him overseas?"

I heard him out.

"I will pay you ten times that sum, but you will earn it the hard way. Here is what you must do." As I outlined my plan, the ship's rat I'd enlisted grew edgy and argued, but I would not be gainsaid. My complicated scheme required, quite rightly, more money than the generous amount I promised the sailor. He needed it to play on the greed of the lowlife infesting the dock area. Some scoundrels will do anything for silver. Thus, we hatched the plot destined to take Edwin to another world.

For it to come to fruition, we had to endure our unwholesome lodgings and food for three days until the weather settled. Our landlord, a former sea-dog, sniffed the air and shook his head. "A gale's brewing, don't be fooled by yon sunshine, Lord." Later, I will reveal why his words pleased me so.

The pre-announced storm broke in the afternoon, bringing lashing waves breaking over the sea defences such as they were. We stayed indoors until it calmed during the night. In the morning, we hastened down to the port to seek out the captain. For once, the dock area did not stink, the stones glistened wet, swept clean by the raging water of the day before. We found our man working on caulking a hull.

"What news?" I accosted him without ado.

"Sunk. Just as you wanted, Lord," he said, knuckling his forehead as seamen do. "Even a sound boat might have sunk in yon storm, but with the one I sent out, they had no chance. Drowned the lot of them, I dare say."

"You dare say? How will we know for sure?"

"Hang about these parts for a few more days." The shrewd, creased face broke into a grin. "There's nought happens in yon stretch of sea," he tilted his head towards the heaving grey waves, "without us knowing."

I groaned at the thought of spending more time in the hovel that passed as an inn. At least the innkeeper offered a decent wine from across the Channel to those like me prepared to pay well for it. Two days later, my informant hurried back to the tavern to find me drinking.

"They got the body, Lord!" was how he greeted me. I waved at him to sit and called for another beaker.

"Yon boat was rotten with age, Lord. Our fellow had the devil's own job to persuade the sewer rats that pass as seamen hereabouts to take her out. Seems there were those as sniffed the storm and our man had to pay way over the odds to get them to cast off. Anyhow, we knew that, but what's new is the body of Edwin and others washed ashore whence they took them to a monastery. They told me the name...hanged if I can remem – ay, that's it, Saint Bert – something or other...Bertin! That's it!"

"How did they know it was Edwin?"

"Simple! A monk from Wintan-caestre recognised him. Appears this fellow was on his way back from pilgrimage and sheltered in the monastery because of the storm."

I grinned at my spy. "Here, sup another, Ingwald, you've earned it! May Edwin drink with the angels and learn some loyalty." I quaffed the red wine, rolling it around my tongue to savour the taste and the prospect of a peaceful West Seax and a return to my comfortable bed. I might not have been quite so jaunty had I known what else was afoot in the land.

I suppose I must have been deluding myself thinking that with Edwin removed, the kingdom of England was consolidated. Not so. The Brittonic underkings, ever rebellious by nature, became restless. The most restless, Constantin of the Scottas, rebelled for the second time in May.

Athelstan called the witan where it was established he would lead a host north overland while I would command a fleet of ships due to my seafaring experience. I would sail from Hamwic, thence up the east coast as far as the great stronghold at Bebbanburgh, there to meet with Athelstan's army.

The settled summer weather helped my voyage, which proved uneventful. We anchored close to the beach in front of the castle and waded ashore at low tide. There we waited for the bad weather to calm before sailing, keeping land in sight, to the far north to a place named Caithness. The Scottas shadowed our every move from the land. When we went ashore, a fight became inevitable. Our battle with the recalcitrant Scottas resulted in an overwhelming victory and the surly re-submission of the King. I advised Athelstan to put an end to the troublemaker, but he would hear of no such thing. He contented himself by showing his might by riding through the land of the Scottas and punishing them where he saw fit. I flatter myself that I can judge a man, and I knew for sure Constantin was not to be trusted.

By October, Athelstan returned to Wintan-caestre. I arrived in September, and Ingwald pleased me with the news that the West Seax nobility appeared in favour of Athelstan. Outwardly, they all spoke well of the King. It is surprising what a good victory can do for a ruler. Not to mention all five Welsh kings agreeing to pay a huge annual tribute. That helped as did his elimination of opposition in ever troublesome Westwealas, right to where the land ends.

Throughout my tale, I have boasted of the rightful importance my help in elevating my nephew to the heights he reached. The consolidation of his reign was down to his virtues, which gained men's love and respect. His law codes strengthened royal control over the now large kingdom. He regulated the weight of silver in the coinage so penalising fraudsters. Buying and selling were, on the whole, confined to the burhs, thus encouraging many to live and work in the well-defended towns. What do people need more than peace and prosperity? Any king who can grant these conditions ensures the loyalty of his subjects. Athelstan became a well-loved ruler. The oddest thing about my nephew, he developed a keenness for collecting religious relics. However, he was smart, giving away many to his followers and to churches to gain their support.

Whether saints' bones, fingernails, and hair brought tranquillity to our land or it was the sensible rule, I cannot say with certainty. Sad to relate, more than these combined blessings and virtues was needed.

Taking advantage of this settled period, I appealed to Athelstan's religious sentiments to allow me time to return to my native Sondwic, explaining my desire to build a church of my own. I knew he would not refuse such a request. Apart from the sacred side of the entreaty, my service and devotion had earned me the right to time away from court.

22

SONDWIC, 933 AD

The period of relative peace we enjoyed this year gave me the opportunity I had long coveted to move forward with my plan to construct a church. To this purpose, I travelled home to Sondwic where, to my dismay, I discovered Father Godfred had died three years before. This came as a severe shock because I loved and trusted my former confessor. My plans, now in fragments, were to follow his advice. His successor, an earnest young fellow named Fremund, showed me Godfred's grave where he led me in prayer before leaving me in silence to relive memories of past times.

When I joined him later, I outlined my plan, which he embraced with unexpected enthusiasm.

"There is a place two leagues to the north-east of here where the folk toil in a dour struggle with the earth. They scratch out a living from the soil that is prone to flooding. I believe it is for this reason their souls are in peril."

"Souls at risk, Father?"

"They are torn between wanting to be righteous Christians, for they are all baptised, and wishing to uphold pagan beliefs.

Would you come with me? I can show you the Land Remedy Charm."

I could scarcely believe my ears. Paganism? Here in Kent? The first place in these isles to convert to Christianity.

"A charm, you say?"

"The proposal of a new church is no coincidence, Lord Ecgwulf. It is inspired by the Lord. Allow me to show you, to understand what I mean."

"Where is this place?"

"By the Little Stour, east of the marsh. But we must arrive there at nightfall."

"Why so?"

"These ignorant folk and their superstitions! They believe the ritual must be performed at night, immediately before daybreak. No matter how I reason with them, they will not forsake this assertion. The Church allows discretion. While it does not tolerate paganism, I can dress these time-hallowed practices in a Christian cloak. Thus, both the church and the villagers are contented. Sometimes I'm not sure whether I'm a priest or a spell-caster!"

"It must be hard for you, Father."

I scrutinised the careworn face of the young man, and I guessed him to have seen one score and five winters. Sorrow tinged the round, florid countenance that looked better suited to merriment. At that moment, I decided I would do anything within my powers to help him drive away the devil from the village hitherto unknown to me.

"When do we go?"

"They wish to begin ploughing straight after Yuletide. We should waste no time."

"Then we shall leave this afternoon."

"A church in the village will mean the salvation of many souls!"

His face lit up for the first time since I had met him. I stared hard into the joyful visage. "Ay, and of mine, that is my firm intention."

We left on horseback, mid-afternoon. To reach the village, we had to skirt marshland, and although the ground was not waterlogged as we approached the village, the turf was springy, and the hoofs of our mounts left imprints behind them.

The priest assured me the land where the village rose was well chosen. I suspect he worried I might change my mind about erecting a church on unsuitable ground.

"Lord Ecgwulf, fear not," he said, "the site was good enough for the Romans. Over there, look!"

I gazed across the weed-infested grassland to a ruined stone building, once a fine villa, no doubt.

"Excellent," I grinned into the anxious countenance of the priest, "stone a-plenty for my church!"

We rode into the village of low, pit-sunk houses thatched with reeds to the cries of excited children running to announce our arrival.

"It's Father Fremund! Father is come with a strange man!"

I grinned wryly, for they didn't know how strange! How could they appreciate I was their lord and master? I, who had been absent all their lifetimes.

My proper importance established, the village headman invited us into his house. Wisely, Father Fremund kept to our agreement not to mention the church project but explained we had come to perform the Land Remedy.

"Tonight it is then!" Our host leapt up and hurried out of the door raising a cry that might have woken the soundest sleeper. "The Land Remedy! The Land Remedy, tonight!" Not that the villagers were destined to sleep well that night. I managed to doze a little, slumber induced by the warmth of the log fire. The damp night-time air came as a strong contrast when the headman led us out by torchlight. We made for the nearest field, a procession of whispering villagers behind. The darkness, according to them, was infested with malign spirits, elves, and ogres. To venture out showed how vital the charm was to them. Their year's supply of food and, thus, survival, depended on Father Fremund working his magic. This explained the presence of the children. Not one person must miss the rite. Two babes in their mothers' arms completed the turnout. I pitied their small shivering bodies, however well their mothers had wrapped them. I heard one father reassure his boy, "Worry not about ogres, we have *the Dane-slayer* with us!"

The ceremony began with four men each cutting a sod of earth from each side of the field. They brought them over to Father Fremund, but later they would be returned to their exact position. The magic cleansing of the turfs ensured the whole field would be cleansed. Women stepped forward in turn to hand the priest the necessary ingredients, which were – *'all known herbs,'* milk from cattle, and twigs from every kind of soft-wood tree. They must have hastened to collect the twigs after the headman had shouted the warning of the ceremony at twilight. I wondered how they had managed. These items, followed by oil, honey, and yeast, the priest placed on top of the cut turfs. Some herbs, not to be found in the winter, were dried and sprinkled in that form. All this symbolised the earth's fruitfulness, and the priest showed the field it must be equally fruitful. He made certain no bewitchment lingered.

To reaffirm the power of the Church and impress the superstitious gathering, he recited *"Crescite, et multiplicamini, et replete, terram,"* – "Grow, and multiply, and replenish the earth." Next, he pronounced, *"In nomine patris et filii et spiritus sancti sitis benedicti."* The sonorous Latin and the flickering torchlight induced, I must admit, a magical atmosphere. It made me shiver with awe, and it was easy for me to imagine how the simple villagers felt. Father Fremund's whisper to me jolted me from my reflections.

"They would have gathered dew in the past for this purpose."

He explained this as he spattered holy water over the turfs from an aspergillum. How surprised I was when the fellow sprinkled it over me as the landowner. The headman of the village pressed aspen wood into my hands and strips of linen. The priest had warned me I would have to make four aspen crosses. He also told me aspen was the wood used for the crucifixion of Christ. Often, he assured me, the villagers threw stones at aspen trees for this reason. What a strange mixture of heathen and Christian were these folk of Stourmouth!

When I consigned the first cross to the priest, he marked it with charcoal, writing the name of Luke, the next with Matthew, then John, and the last with Mark, thus representing each of the gospels.

"The cross stands for the sun wheel," the village headman announced as if to correct a misinterpretation of the ritual.

The priest placed the crosses on the turfs repeating "*Crescite*" nine times: nine, a magical number.

He then proceeded to declare:

Eastward I stand, for blessings I pray,
I pray the mighty Lord, I pray the potent Prince,
I pray the holy guardian of the celestial realm,
Earth, I pray, and heaven above,
And the just and saintly Mary...

The prayer continued for a time with invocations and ended with:

...That no witch so artful, nor seer so cunning be
That e'er may overturn the words hereto pronounced.

At the word *witch,* I shuddered and recalled the sorceress we had drowned years ago. For a moment, I was overcome by irrational fear of what lay beyond the flickering confines of the light cast by the flaming, smoking torch. I cannot say I was displeased when the men replaced the turfs, the rite ended, and we trudged back to the houses.

The next procedure for the charm was due to take place when ploughing began. Depending on the weather, it should be in a week's time. I needed to be there and was happy to please the expectant villagers. Good relations with the village would aid in expediting the plans for my church.

In the village came the most curious part of the ceremony. The only person left in the settlement was a beggar leaning on a wooden crutch. The village headman hastened to him and demanded, "Give me the seeds!"

Whether what followed was a recital to fit the part, I know not, but suspect it so. The beggar shook his head and hid something behind his back.

"Take it from him, lads!"

Three men pounced on the beggar, one bracing him to stop his fall. The others wrested a bag of seeds from him.

"Would you steal from a poor beggar?" the wretch wailed.

"Looks like we will!" the village headman glanced at me with a nervous expression.

"All's well," whispered the priest, "they will give him back twice what they took. It is the ritual. Thus, the seeds will thrive because they are stolen. Giving back the double the amount of seed magically increases the land's fertility to yield double the weight of crops."

"I see," I said, incredulous at these superstitions. If it pleased the ceorls, that was what mattered until they became true Christians.

I rode to the village a week later. For the next part of the spell, as landowner, I had to gather ploughing implements and bore a hole into the beam of the plough. This showed to everyone that my involvement in the magical process was not performed purely on my behalf. Into the bored hole, I placed incense, fennel, hallowed soap, and salt, and, finally, the stolen seed.

At last, the ploughing began and my involvement in the rite was finished. Whatever I thought at the time about the ancient ceremony, I had to admit at the time of harvest, the yield was plentiful. Praise the Lord!

Before my horse carried me back to Sondwic, I spoke at length with the village headman about my project for a church in the village. He was obliged to accept since the land and the decision were mine. His local knowledge proved indispensable, for I sought a place close to the houses but raised enough to not be subject to flooding in the winter. Such a location, he showed me, and I paced out the size of the church and marked it out with hazel twigs.

I wanted a cruciform church with a central tower. This idea came to me from another church seen on my travels, where the local people fled and took refuge in the tower to escape from a Viking raid. Our land was still not free of the scourge of the Norsemen. The Stour estuary had always been a natural approach for raiders from the North Sea, so a man could never be too cautious. For this reason, I wanted such a tower in my church.

Stone walls built of local flint dressing the Roman stones salvaged from the ruins was what I envisaged. I gave instructions for them to be carried to the site, a few at a time, when men could be spared from the working fields or from fishing. My task would be to go to Lunden where I was sure to find a master mason: I wanted *my* church to be well constructed.

Discreet inquiries in Lunden bore fruit. I sat before a jocular, square-faced mason who filled my head with many terms I did not understand. He was forced to lead me to his current workplace, a church near the River Fleta. Opening a lock to a small wooden hut with a key as long as my hand, he showed me drawings of the pilaster strips, blank arcading, baluster shafts, and triangular headed openings that in his earlier speech had been so much gibberish to my bewildered brain. With the aid of these sketches, his terminology became clear, and I could see that Providence had led me to the right man.

Outside the edifice he was working on, I pointed out what I wanted and did not want. The church I contemplated would be smaller than this, though not by much, but I insisted on the central tower over the nave. This meant more money. When I told him it was not an impediment, he became more amenable. In practical terms, it involved constructing the tower around split oak trunks.

"I saw such a church," I told him.

"Oh, ay, where?"

"A place called Derehurst, near Glevcaestre."

The hearty laugh startled me.

"I worked on yon when I learnt my trade as an apprentice!"

"So, you will understand what I want, I have no doubt."

"We can start as soon as you like. I have men with little left to do here. The carpenters will soon be busier than the rest. The roof beams have to be positioned and then the thatching, and we're done here."

"I can take with me whoever you think fit to see the site:"

"I'll come along too, so as I can organise the purchase of stone and wood and ensure there are no problems for the foundations. Yon part of the world's a devil for underground streams and the like."

All arrangements made, I, Ecgwulf Ealheresson, Ealdorman of Sondwic, beamed and clasped hands with the master mason. Work would start on the foundations the next day, and this stretch of abandoned ground to be cleared of weeds and brambles before sunset would change forever. I hoped to return often to check on progress, but I supposed my King would need me in his Council meetings and, more urgently, on his battlefields.

With a heavy heart, I left the scir of my infancy and rode to Witan-caestre, where grave news awaited me. This I will relate in a further account. Suffice it to say, it kept me away from Stourmouth for a twelvemonth and two more moons. When I returned, I was amazed at the sight to meet my delighted eyes. The structure was almost completed.

I turned to the master mason who greeted me with his usual cheerful humour. "What do you think, Lord Ecgwulf?"

"I did not expect such rapid progress, my friend." I clapped him on the back.

"It's surprising what having ready money gets you. The labourers I needed to do the lifting and build the scaffolding were never in short supply. The men of the village, used to a hard life of poverty, prove more than willing to work for pay. They're taking much pride in their new church, you know."

"What is there still to be done?"

"The last level of the tower, one more floor, the refinement around the door and the windows. Let me show you the sketches." He led the way to a wooden hut he used as an office. On the table lay a roll of parchment. The mason unfurled and flattened it out. He pointed to the enlarged drawing of a window. "Here, either side of the round-arched window, I want to position these stone strips running down the wall and on them false columns with bases, as in the drawing."

"They serve no purpose?"

"No purpose, Lord! The purpose is to beautify! Do they not please the eye?"

"They do."

"To finish off the work on the door," he rolled the parchment back further, "a perfect round arch but with a carved moulding. It ought to offset the wall's knapped flint well. What do you say to a head? Over the door arch, I mean."

"A head? Why, have we captured a Viking?"

The mason shook with laughter. "Bless you, Lord, of course not! I meant a sculpted head. Who is the church to be dedicated to? Is there any particular saint?"

I had to confess, in my religious profanity, I had not thought of this. A church needs a dedication. But I had no special saint I called upon.

"Nay, master, I'm going to need all the saints I can get my hands on to save my soul. I can't limit myself to one. That's no good."

"*All Saints*, is it?" The master grinned. "Not enough room above the door in that case. We'd need all the wall space and more besides! It seems there's a new saint every day."

That is how I decided on the dedication at Stourmouth.

"Course, we could put the carved head of Our Lord above the door," the mason said. He seemed reluctant and disconsolate at renouncing his idea.

"Do it!"

Within the year's end, the church was finished, inside and out. It cost me a fair sum, but I could afford it. The joy on the faces of the villagers when the new bell chimed out the first mass remains with me to this day, etched on my memory. Dedication of All Saints took place on a Sunday. Father Fremund participated, although, for such an occasion, it was Archbishop Wulfhelm who conducted the service. He, it was who led the procession, crozier held high before us to the church from the simple wooden cross in the village where services had been held in all weathers. We marched behind him singing and praying into the church. *My* church.

The first ritual was the handing over. The mason and I

knelt before the archbishop and together raised a cushion bearing the key. Next, the archbishop blessed the water and sprinkled the people gathered in the church, for they, he told them, were the spiritual temple. When he had done with wetting everyone, he proceeded to the walls, and finally, the altar.

There followed the usual readings and hymns and a homily delivered by Archbishop Wulfhelm. Who better to get my church off to a fine start? It culminated in a litany of saints. Most appropriate, I thought, keen to keep as many saints on my side as possible. The Eucharist incorporated a prayer of dedication and the anointing of the altar with chrism. Father Fremund covered the altar with a white linen cloth then lit candles and the mass ended.

The sense of relief I felt shames me. As a man of action, I found the service tedious, but upon calm reflection, I understood the importance of due ceremonial to the heathen folk of my village. With their own church to unite the community in faith, every important event from baptism to inhumation would be under the sign of the Cross. I swelled with pride – a deadly sin – and made my way back to less secluded and more violent circumstances.

23

WINTAN-CAESTRE, 930-937 AD

Athelstan crushed the revolt in the long peninsula of Westwealas, stretching toward the great ocean, ensuring peace. With the leaders of Gwent, Dyfed, and Powys frequent visitors to our court, the seven-year period from 930 was one of relative quiet. Our retinue, constantly on the move in search of food, stayed, for the most part, in West Seax. King Alfred had ruled with a small group of advisers, but my nephew's Witan grew bigger due to the expansion of the kingdom.

The King set great store by education, founding a chapel school and contacting Frankia and other countries overseas. The academy produced fine manuscripts and trained scholars. This learning helped to expedite the formulation of six law codes.

I have spent much of my tale relating how Athelstan became King and my part in this, but I ought to tell how he consolidated his reign. Thus, I have to relive years passed. Athelstan's mother was King Edward's first wife, but then he married two women who bore many children. This, as Athelstan was quick to realise, meant he disposed of the asset of several half-sisters. How better to enhance his own importance than by marrying them to the princes of Europe?

This began in 919 when Eadgifu wed the West Frankish King, Charles the Simple. Eleven years later, wishing to stake a claim to equality and seal an alliance between the two Seax kingdoms, the German King, the elderly Henry, contacted Athelstan. He sought a wife of noble lineage for his grandson, Otto. Confident of a positive reply, Henry dispatched a well-armed delegation to accompany the princess back to his native land. I expect they served to guard the opulent gifts he sent! It must be the reason why I was not chosen to escort the pretty Eadgyth to Germany. I will admit to disappointment since I had never ventured overseas.

With Eadgyth, Athelstan dispatched her sister, Edgiva, to Germany. Henry instructed his eldest son and heir to the throne, Otto, to choose whichever one pleased him best. Otto chose Eadgyth, a woman of pure noble countenance, graceful character and truly royal appearance. He wed her in 930. Edgiva, instead, married Louis, brother of King Rudolf of Burgundy. Steadily, the prestige of Athelstan grew with each of these unions.

In 926 an embassy arrived from Athelstan's cousin, Adelof, Count of Boulogne, on behalf of Hugh, Duke of the Franks. It was hard to believe my eyes when the gifts appeared in the hall before him. Perfumes and spices from the orient, the like of which I had never smelt and which made my head spin. Jewels sparkled red, green, and blue in an alabaster vase – the first time I had seen such whiteness. To the king's delight, he received the sword of Emperor Constantine with the spear of Charlemagne and a part of the Crown of Thorns. What I coveted most whinnied outdoors – six fine horses with trappings. Seeing my yearning eyes, Athelstan gave me the choice of a fine animal, and I selected the dappled grey stallion.

This magnificence did not come without a request: a bride for Hugh. This time, Athelstan chose his half-sister, Eadhild. Let me explain. These gracious princesses were but pawns in a political game, whose movements I do not understand. But Athelstan told me that Adelof needed to put down a challenge for the throne of Frankia by separating Hugh from the dangerous Heribert of Vermandois. What better way than offering him an irresistible Seax princess in exchange for his alliance? In spite of my earnest pleas, I was again passed over for the journey across the seas I so longed for. But my time would come.

Meanwhile, Eadgifu bore Charles a babe named Louis. In 922, Count Heribert of Vermandois seized the King, imprisoned, and deposed him. The following year, Eadgifu fled with her young son to Wintan-caestre to protect the boy's safety. Athelstan did not conceal his delight and added Louis to his two fosterlings, half-brothers by his father's third wife, Edmund and Eadred.

Athelstan collected books and relics that I never understood but, more to my taste, loved hunting, falconry, and practising his skills with the sword. He encouraged the three boys in these interests, and they grew strong and learned in his court. Athelstan never married or sired children, but these were as good as sons to him, and he a loving father to them. It was as if he had an unspoken agreement with Eadgifu: he would have no children, and she and her sons would cause him no dynastic problems. But their relationship went beyond this. She organised his dress, so the King was always immaculate in appearance, and undertook many other domestic arrangements.

In my old age, I look back on these years as the happiest of my life also because, at last, my chance came to visit the continent. Little did I know that luck was on my side because dark war clouds were gathering. The storm did not break, however, until I was back safely in West Seax.

First, I will relate my journey overseas. In spring 936, a messenger arrived from Frankia from the Margrave of Neustria, the famous, mighty Hugh the Great. Unknown to us, King Charles died in captivity, so his son Louis became the only male heir to the throne – he boasted six half-sisters! The message was simple. *"Come and take the head of the kingdom."*

Athelstan, by now a wise and imposing ruler and anything but ingenuous, forced the ambassadors to kneel and bend over many sainted relics. He constrained them to swear solemn oaths that the future king would have the homage of all his vassals. Not until these vows were taken would he allow Louis and his mother to depart his court. This was the extent of his love for the young man, as I said, regarded with a father's loving eye. Such was this fondness, he decided, to my great joy, to send *the Dane-slayer* as an escort.

"Let nothing harmful befall my nephew!" He clutched my arm with such ferocity when he uttered these words that I winced.

We travelled with three bishops and a number of Louis and Eadgifu's faithful servants to land on the beach of Boulogne. The crossing tested my stomach, but I did not let it show to my companions, unaffected by the motion of the ship. Could a renowned warrior reveal himself to be weaker than a bishop or a princess?

As the bows crunched into the shell-littered beach, Louis shook off hands proffered in assistance and leapt into the shallow foaming waves. I hastened after him, and there, on the strand, Louis received the homage of Hugh and a few Frankish nobles, who one by one knelt and kissed his hand. I shall never forget what followed. The Duke brought a horse decorated with the royal insignia. When he wanted to put the King in the saddle, the creature ran in all directions; but Louis, an agile young man, jumped suddenly, without stirrups, and tamed the animal. This pleased all those present and earned recognition from all.

After my introduction and that of Eadgifu, although Hugh knew her from former days at court, we trudged over the sand to where a carriage awaited her and her maids. They gave me a horse, less spirited than Louis's, and we rode to a place called Laon. There the coronation was to take place at the Abbey of Notre-Dame, so Louis told me, for he was born in that town and it was his express wish.

On Sunday, the nineteenth day of June, 936, the Archbishop of Rems, in the presence of twenty bishops, crowned Louis the fourth of his name as King. I say, for certain, the young King cut a splendid figure, wearing a blue silk coat called *Orbis Terrarum* with cosmic allusions, as worn by his ancestor Charles the Bald. His purple robe was encrusted with precious stones and gold. The unfolding story of Louis is well worth telling, but for me, it ends here. Duty done, I made my way back to the coast and embarked for my homeland, content to have seen something, however little, of the wider world beyond its shores.

In Wintan-caestre, the news from our spies that greeted me was not to my liking. Filled with resentment, Constantin of the Scottas had woven a web of alliances to retaliate for his defeat and Athelstan's riding with impunity around his kingdom in 934. Nearing three-score years of age, I was becoming used to the peaceful life, but I could not forsake my nephew in his hour of need. The challenge that faced us was severe if our informants were to be believed. An old foe reared his vengeful head, and I do not refer to Constantin but to Gofraid, or rather, his son. The Viking King of Dublin, who we had driven out of Eoforwic, had stirred hatred for Athelstan in his offspring, Olaf, now King after his father's death two years before. Olaf Gofraidsson gathered a host and sailed for the Mersey. There, he met with Constantin and King Owen of Strathclyde. The threat, mighty as it was, could only be faced head-on.

I swore I was too old for this game, but I covered myself in glory in spite of my advanced age as a warrior. By contrast, we took the youthful Edmund, who insisted on fighting beside his half-brother. We advanced north-west with a force composing the men of West Seax, Mierce, Danes, and Wealisc. Had ever such an unlikely alliance been forged to defend our land against invaders? But that is what occurred as we marched to endure the most important battle ever fought in these Isles.

24

CAITHNESS, ALBA, JULY 934 AD

H ead reeling, Constantin stared at the dust-covered rider, whose anguished face he found hard to interpret. Did he read fear underlying the woe? In that case, the news must be dire.

"Fear not, friend," Constantin reassured him, "be calm and relate what you have to tell."

"Sire, we proceeded north for days, keeping the English ships within sight, for they never sailed out on the high seas but stayed in range of vision of our lands. They reached the northernmost outposts of your kingdom, Lord, before they landed with their horses and wagons."

A growl escaped Constantin's mouth, and his countenance grew thunderous. The news bearer hesitated, anxious.

"Go on!"

"Lord Ildulb gave the order to pitch camp, for we would attack at first light. He hoped to catch the foe by surprise, for as you know, dawn comes early in this season, up there, but–"

"But?"

"Betrayal, Sire! Our scouts caught a Scot leaving the enemy encampment. Before he died, he confessed he had warned Athelstan of our presence and the dawn attack. The English stayed on guard all night, waiting ready for us."

Constantin leapt to his feet and, with great self-restraint, refrained from seizing the messenger, "Who?" he bellowed. "Who sent the traitor?"

The man glanced around the room, his unease palpable. He leant towards his King and whispered, "Lord Ildulb commanded me to speak this name, Sire: Màel Coluim mac Domnaill."

The messenger stepped back out of reach of his monarch whose wrathful countenance twisted with hatred. The emissary believed his King's rage destined to grow far worse and wished he were anywhere in the kingdom but there. The rest of his communication might unleash a terrible reaction. He gazed at the sword hanging at the King's side, and beads of sweat dampened his brow. Not delivering his message would be graver than consigning it. What a plight!

Before King Constantin exploded into verbal outrage and abuse, he interceded. "Sire, I am but a messenger. I crave your mercy. There is more to tell, forgive me."

"Ay," Constantin held his fury in check and considered the difficult lot of a purveyor of bad news. The wretched servant was not to blame. "Get on with it, man! No-one in his right mind would punish an innocent bearer of news."

It did not reassure the perspiring Scot. Constantin did not appear to be master of his mind and might lose control at the next words.

"Sire, defeat! Lord Ildulb's army fought bravely, but the English had more men and without surprise—"

"I-is Ildulb alive?"

"Ay, Sire, and on his way here."

"The Lord be praised!"

"There is more..."

"Well?"

"Your firstborn grandson, Amlaib, died at the hands of the aetheling Edmund. I'm deeply sorry, Lord."

A howl echoed from the rafters, and Constantin crashed a fist on a table to vent his rage. The English would pay for this, by God, one day, they would! So would Màel Coluim...one day. The loss was his fault. For the moment, the traitor boasted a strong position, a sizeable group of families backed him, but Constantin knew how to bide his time.

This was, indeed, a useful attribute because, six weeks later, a summons to the court of the English King arrived. Constantin considered himself too weak to refuse the command. Obeying it meant resubmission, but what could he do? Another defeat to the arrogant Athelstan would have unthinkable consequences for his reign. Now fomented by Màel Coluim's whisperings, the word abdication hung in the air. He had no choice but to make the week-long journey to Cyrneceaster.

In September, unimpressed, Constantin entered the Hall in that town with a sneer on his face at this royal vill smaller than his own palace. Nothing more than a glorified farmhouse, it was surrounded by barns. Inside the hall, flowers in vases spaced around worsened his mood. He preferred walls full of hanging axes and spears. In this way, it felt as if Athelstan were mocking him: Constantin conquered by a flower-lover!

Athelstan greeted him with cordiality and pleasantries, but his eyes hardened and, with formalities over, so did his words.

"King Constantin, I rode through your lands and admired the vastness and the wealth of resources you can call upon.

How is it I have not received the tithe we agreed upon at Eamont?"

The face of the King of the Scottas, lined and wrinkled, twisted into a grotesque mask. The fearsome glower that caused men in his kingdom to quail before him had little effect, if not the contrary, on Athelstan, who laughed outright.

"Come now, King Constantin, there is no call to transform your noble features into the semblance of a demon. We must discuss what tribute you will send south before winter sets in."

"I know not what you think you saw, but mine is a poor realm, and we are hard-pressed to meet our needs."

"Then you must press harder, Constantin, else you will possess no country, rich or poor, to call your own."

This English brat will pay for that remark. He will not be smiling when the Scottas descend on his lands and lay them waste!

Such thoughts consoled Constantin, but his visage showed no similar malice. Revenge would be sweet when it came, but for now, he needed to buy time. What was the English king saying?

"...and such fine long-horned, shaggy-coated cattle roaming free. Not to mention the vast acres of woodland?"

Athelstan looked as if he required an answer, but Constantin had been distracted. He ground his teeth and peering at the younger monarch, said, "Get on with it then!" He did not suppose it to be the right response, but it expressed what he wanted most, to end this farce and to return to Alba.

The rite of resubmission, a painful process for Constantin, involved a pledge to pay gold and cede timber and cattle. The upstart made it clear that not fulfilling his agreement meant invasion and dethronement. The act of making his mark became the hardest thing the King of the Scottas had ever performed. Constantin told himself he was signing a declaration of war, one he alone knew about. This thought enabled him to give Athelstan a wry smile and clasp hands when he straightened his back. One day, he would teach the arrogant Englishman the cost of riding uninvited through his kingdom with impunity.

25

THE WIRRAL, OCTOBER 737 AD

Constantin bit his tongue. He refused to tell Olaf the Viking that he should not trust the word of Vikings, for it would be an unwise move. The King's network of informants had assured him that these mercenaries standing before them were in the pay of Athelstan. The Skallagrimsson brothers were bold deceivers, and their silver tongues persuaded Olaf because he spoke the same language: not only that of silver but also of gold. Emissaries of the spineless Seax, they offered it by the wagonload to avoid a fight and to make their enemy go. Constantin was convinced of trickery.

At last, he persuaded Olaf to listen to his argument somewhere they could not be overheard.

"My spies insist Athelstan is far from the Wirral. It's a trick to buy time. Do not forget our original purpose to surprise the Angles and to march swiftly to take Caestir. We are losing the element of surprise. We must not delay. Refuse their inducement and give the order to leave!"

The Viking King of Dublin glowered at the old Scot who presumed to tell him what to do.

"You will not decide for us all. I will give the other leaders their say. The proposition is good, and we shall discuss it."

Olaf called the meeting, and although tempted, the other leaders decided to reject the offer and demanded more gold.

The envoys exchanged glances, and Constantin bridled. He did not trust them in the slightest. One of the brothers, Egil by name, bowed to Olaf saying, "Lord, I beg for time to take this proposal to King Athelstan for our king to consider and respond. He is but a day's journey to the south with a *mighty host*." He stressed the last words with a satisfied smirk and Constantin bunched his fist.

Olaf agreed to a three-day truce.

"Very well," Olaf consented, "you shall have three days; otherwise, battle commences."

The Icelandic brothers left with their escort to expedite the mission. Constantin glared at Olaf.

"You fell straight into their trap. Don't say you weren't warned."

"What makes you so sure it was a trap?"

"I sent scouts to find Athelstan's army. Let me tell you, none of them returned. I must suppose they were captured and slain. We do not have information, only the word of these *Vikings!*" Constantin fair spat the last word.

"Watch your tongue if you value it, old man!"

Constantin paled at the murderous glint in Olaf's eyes. The Norseman would not have dared to address him in that tone twenty years ago. He was old, but unlike Olaf, he still had his wits about him. They told him not to trust the guileful envoys.

They reappeared three days later, offering the original amount once more. At the outraged reaction of Olaf and Constantin, the other Skallagrimsson brother, Thorolf, paused for a moment.

"Our King will give you an additional scillingas to every freeborn man. He will add a silver mark to every officer of a company of twelve men or more, a gold mark to every captain of the King's guard, and five gold marks to every jarl."

Constantin's heart sank as greed lit up the eyes of the King of Dublin.

"We must call a conference to discuss this matter," Olaf rose from his seat, "await our decision."

What followed was not a genuine discussion, Constantin brooded, more a coercion.

"Think what use we'll make of this money in our homelands," Olaf said. "In Ireland, we can raise a mighty force to expand westwards; no-one will be able to resist us."

"What about the English? Taking their gold will not weaken them," Constantin pointed out.

At last, Ealdred of Bernicia found his voice. "They are still on our doorstep, King Olaf. What happened to your much-vaunted claim to the Kingdom of Jorvik? Was it not taken from your family by this English King?"

"By Thor, you are right!" Ealdred had touched a raw nerve. "Without the surrender of Jorvik, it's war!"

Ignoring the correct formalities custom demanded, Olaf stormed out of the meeting without another word.

He left the envoys in no doubt as to his vile mood. "If your King grants me the overlordship of Northanhymbre and keeps his pledge about the gold, we shall return home. He has three days truce to decide.

"And," Constantin's voice made Olaf spin round, "my emissaries will accompany you back to your King for his answer. Is that clear?"

The King of the Scottas scrutinised the faces of the wily Skallagrimsson brothers but did not see the doubt or worry he expected. They agreed, unfazed. Still, Constantin did not feel reassured. His gut feeling was one of wariness against trickery. The English King had gained a whole seven days from Olaf. A week wisely used would have seen them installed in Caestir by now with the south at their mercy. Respect was lacking in this alliance: respect for his greater experience and wisdom. Once more, his spies had failed to return, but this was a sure way of learning the whereabouts of the King Athelstan. With a wry smile and persistent disgruntlement, he accompanied the envoys out of the tent.

"You may have fooled Olaf, but you don't fool me," he murmured to Egil Skallagrimsson, who took his leave with a bow and a mocking grin that did nothing to reassure the Scot.

Athelstan's forced march had brought him to within half a day's journey from the heath where the battle, if it were to be fought, would take place. He was quick to receive the emissaries from Constantin.

"Tell your King we reject Olaf's terms and demand the coalition withdraw from Northanhymbre and return to their own lands. First, he must restore the booty he has thus far taken on the campaign." Athelstan spoke in a cold, measured voice deliberately adding insult to injury.

"Furthermore, the cost of peace will be borne by King Olaf and the other coalition leaders who will become my vassals, ruling their lands as my under-kings."

The emissaries of King Constantin, dour men all, kept their feelings hidden but quaked inwardly at the thought of the message they must deliver to their irascible monarch.

Wise as he was, Constantin did not release his temper on his own men but channelled his fury at Olaf.

"Did I not tell you it was nought but a ploy to gain time? Athelstan is almost here with a mighty host." He curbed his wrath since he could not defeat the English alone. "Come, we must not quarrel among ourselves. United, we will overcome our enemy and make him pay for his arrogance."

"We will do that, for sure. To the heath before first light! We shall surprise the curs."

26

BRUNANBURH, OCTOBER 937 AD

The might of West Seax and Mierce stretched out behind us in the form of our elite fyrd. the enemy had sailed from Dublin, from the Western Isles, and from Strathclyde to form a vast fleet. So, it was a comfort to have such men at our backs.

We needed reassurance because yesterday afternoon our plans became confounded. An abrupt change of direction forced us to think again. We were sure the Norse invasion would come through the well-worn Danish route of the five boroughs to the east. But we had reckoned without the cunning of Olaf Gofraidsson. We knew he intended to reclaim his 'birthright,' the 'kingdom of Jorvik,' which he maintains Athelstan stole from his father. Why would we expect an attack from the west? Owing to the foresight of Aethelflaed and her network of informants, we received news of the arrival of the first enemy ships on the Wirral peninsula. It is a place where the Mersey on one side and the Dee on the other shape the land.

As we rode, Athelstan and I discussed the situation.

"Why come to the west?" I voiced my perplexity.

Athelstan grinned at me from his saddle. There was no happiness in a smile that expressed satisfaction at understanding the enemy's guile.

"Much safer than sailing around the far north at this time of year. You never know when a squall might blow up."

"Why on the Wirral?"

"Did you leave your brain behind in Witan-caestre?"

There was humour in his grin, and I scowled at him in exchange.

"I don't see it," I confessed. "It's a hard march from there to Eoforwic."

"I hope your arm is stronger than your head, Uncle!"

"If you were not my King with thousands of men behind you, I'd show you," I growled, irritated by his mocking.

"Forgive me," said he, used to my ever-present good nature and disturbed by this display of rancour. "Follow my reasoning, which is sure to be theirs. The Wirral is near Caestir. It is October and the harvest, a rich one this year, is gathered in. The granaries are replete. In Caestir, Olaf has many supporters, some capable of opening the gates to his force. Caestir is also the home of the royal mint and my silver. If the enemy takes the town, the way is open to press into the heart of Mierce and thence into Wessex. Are you with me, Ecgwulf?"

He saw my eyes glaze over but not from lack of attention, more from the effort of taking in and extending his argument with its consequences.

He was right. Why undertake the wearisome march over the Pennines when a rich prize was to hand? If Caestir fell, Olaf could negotiate the restitution of Eoforwic from a position of strength. Constantin of the Scottas would be free of his obligations to the English throne, without question.

"Well, Uncle?"

"Once again you are right, my King. We must hasten to prevent such an eventuality."

"That is why I dispatched riders at dawn to the fortresses of Rumcofan and Thelwall to strengthen their fyrds. It's as well I followed my aunt's example and kept their garrisons at full strength. I sent word to the local thegns in Northern Mierce to raise men. We will meet with them all to swell our ranks."

"Is there anything you haven't thought of, Nephew?"

For once, he looked anxious and sounded less secure.

"Our informants speak of ninety-eight ships in the enemy fleet."

"Ninety-eight!" I hissed, whistling through my teeth as I made a swift calculation. "Seven thousand men or more."

"And war-hardened. They've fought in their own lands without ceasing these last few years. Thank goodness, not all their ships are fast. Only a dozen or so have moored in the pool known as Wallesey. They must wait for the slower vessels to arrive and, God willing, this will allow us time to cut off their advance on Caestir."

I lapsed into silence while I had a thought.

"Is the land to the south of the Dee not marshy?"

"But many Norsemen live on the peninsula. Do not forget the campaign Aethelflaed waged to subdue them. There will be guides a-plenty willing to lead them across the treacherous ground."

"Blast their eyes!"

I fell silent once more, but the King brought me back to the present.

"I have paid Viking mercenaries to fight for us. As we talk, they have marked out the battlefield with hazel sticks as custom dictates, and they will fool the enemy by pitching camp there and having all their men sleep on the ground outside their tents."

"Outside! That's clever!"

"Ecgwulf, I see your brain has returned."

"In that way, they it will look as if there are not enough tents for so many men. As if the encampment is overflowing."

"I have made another decision."

His tone captured my complete attention, a strange mixture, authoritative yet worried.

"For the battle, which there will no doubt be, I will command the centre of our army. You will lead our men against the enemy's weakest flank to turn it. But that will not be your most important task..."

Athelstan twisted to look at the aetheling Edmund riding at his other side. His half-brother insisted on accompanying us, with the unexpected blessing of his mother, the intelligent Eadgifu. She quashed any misgivings she may have felt in favour of the benefits to be gained to enhance Edmund's reputation. The aetheling boasted but ten and seven winters. His battle skills, well-honed by me and Athelstan, no-one could dispute, but facing tempered warriors in the shield wall was a different matter from practising combat in a courtyard, and this worried the king. He turned back to me, "...which will be to protect my brother and make sure he lives to return to Witancaestre. Will you do that for me, Uncle?"

I smiled into the tense face of my King. How could he wage a battle if his thoughts centred on protecting his brother?

"Of course, Lord, I will defend him with all my strength and my last drop of blood."

I watched the tension disappear from Athelstan's countenance. He nodded and pointed to his baggage train. "I have brought an altar and relics. With your arm and my prayers, he will be safe."

We camped for the night, and Athelstan prayed. I drank mead and chatted with some ealdormen about the oncoming war. I do not know who of the two of us prepared better, but I woke with a clear head and devised a cunning scheme. We distanced a half-day's march from the Wirral at this point when I broached my suggestion to Athelstan. He accepted it with the eagerness of a keen mind. The best ploys are often startling in their simplicity. Mine was to send a Dane, since we had many among our number, ahead to report on our approach. His message to the enemy would be to reassure them that only a local thegn and his war-band were advancing, not the whole of the Miercian and West Seaxa force.

By mid-afternoon, this deceitful communication lured the Norsemen into moving swiftly across the Roman road, past the small settlement of Storeton. They had the advantage of the terrain, attacking our vanguard downhill. We had the benefit of surprise, but not at first. A savage skirmish began, man to man, without a shield wall. The weight of their attack forced us back, but then came the unexpected arrival of Athelstan with the main force to support us. We had held firm, but now we drove the enemy to retreat beyond Storeton, where they awaited the coming of Kings Olaf and Constantin. We regrouped and set up a camp close to the watch post of another local thegn, Bruna, who was eager to join us with his men. We rested for what was left of the day and the night, wary of an early morning arrack by our wily adversary.

In the late afternoon, we were glad to be joined by the local fyrds from Caestir, Rumcofan, Eddisbury, and as far afield as Nametwic. My rough estimate of our forces amounted to eight thousand men, so we more than matched the number of enemies.

Our scouts reported on the lie of the land. Before daylight lit up our surroundings, our ears pricked to the sound of movement outside the encampment. The first warnings called, we dressed in haste. I pulled on my mail shirt and found my thick leather gloves and helm.

Athelstan appeared at my tent already prepared for battle, his shield hanging across his back.

"Now they know our true strength, what do you think they will do?"

"I don't suppose they will retreat. Olaf won't want to lose face, will he? In any case, I doubt he'd be able to assemble such a force again were he to leave. No, he will attack to push on to Caestir."

"I agree. I'll offer negotiations to dupe them," Athelstan's eyes hardened, "but I'll brook no agreement with the oath-breaker—"

"Constantin." It was not a question.

He spat at the mention of the cunning Scot's name. "If we pretend to negotiate, more of our men will arrive in the time gained."

"They may think we are afraid," I offered.

"They can imagine what they will."

The dawn revealed the Norsemen drawn up into position, one flank protected by the Clatterbrook. This was a wise tactic by our foe to protect himself beside a babbling stream. My experienced eye swept over the enemy ranks: they were better equipped and trained than us, but we outnumbered them. Not satisfied with our greater numbers, Athelstan sent a delegation to treat with Olaf and Constantin. He did this to buy time, but I grew restless, yearning to commence the fight. The deception gained us more men but otherwise proved fruitless. The emissaries withdrew, and insults and desultory arrows flew, the latter falling short as the enemy archers stood well back in reserve.

A short war council with Edmund, the leading ealdormen and thegns, the mercenaries, Athelstan and I, led to taking decisions. There was no point in attacking the enemy's left flank in strength because of the stream, but enough men must descend on them to stop reinforcement of the central shield wall. That was the target of our well-trained Miercian and West Seaxa fyrds who, under Athelstan's command, formed into a shield wall. Instead, the King ordered Edmund and me together with Thorolf Skallagrimsson to assault the right flank bordered by a small wooded rise. Our aim would be to turn that flank and roll it up. All the arrangements agreed, unknown to us, Constantin had sent men to hide among the trees in the case of any such attempt on our part.

Our undoing was the view we had of the battle from the rising ground leading into the woods. The din of the shield walls coming together, the clash of metal on metal, the cries, and screams, all made for a fascinating spectacle. It distracted us so much the first we knew of the enemy hidden in the undergrowth was their savage surprise attack. It cost us many men and much ground to javelins as they forced us backwards. I remember it as if it were today:

In the heat of battle, I still manage to note our adversaries, so different from us in appearance. They are all shapes and sizes, various hair colours and mixed shield patterns and clothing. We have the same hues on our shields and dress alike. They fight the same as us, the same weapons, the same strength. It strikes me that the slaughter will be terrible. Only subterfuge might overcome an equal enemy and their first manoeuvre gives them the advantage. Bishop Odo, to my left, realises this. Spattered in the blood of his victims, he shouts to me that he will seek help, for our plight is grave. Thorolf Skallagrimsson falls, hacked down by a Viking jarl.

I hear the enemy leader exhort his men to greater effort. I know it not, but this is Gebeachan, King of the Western Isles. I growl to a thegn by my side to guard Edmund with his life, though I fear more for the Norsemen attacking Edmund, who is acquitting himself with distinction. Strength redoubled by rage, for I cannot contemplate defeat, even in this skirmish far from the shield wall, I hack my way toward the stocky figure of their leader. He is fresh because he, busy directing operations, has not yet struck a blow in anger. He smirks and sneers, inviting me towards him with a series of insults which serve only to increase my wrath. It is a cold seething fury because a man can afford no other type on the battlefield, where one over-rash move can cost him his life.

I close on Gebeachan who stokes my wrath by tossing his shield to the ground to face me with an axe and a sword. He beckons me on, but I need no invitation. My eyes lock on his feet because how they shift will tell me the nature of his attack. His weight is on his front foot, but the other steps forward, and I feint to his left and dodge to his right. He has no time to adjust his balance as *Breath Stealer* slices under his axe arm and bites through the leather of his jerkin into the flesh. I twist the blade, and he winces. He's too proud to scream.

In a trice, his sword is flashing towards my neck, but I'm ready and my shield goes up to take this blow followed in an instant by another from his axe. This jars my arm, and I'm surprised at the strength of the wounded man. Another terrible blow from the same weapon judders up my arm. My shield is old and tempered in battle, it will not shatter, but it seizes the axe-head in its wooden grip. I take advantage, wrenching the protective barrier so the haft of the axe twists in his clasp and unbalances him. He realises the folly of disposing of his own shield as his left flank is exposed to my lunging blade. It drives through the leather in the same place as the first wound. This time, he howls and slumps to the ground on one knee. I lean all my weight on my sword and watch the life fade from his eyes.

Oblivious to the battle raging around me until this moment,

my frantic glances tell me that Bishop Odo has succeeded in sending our reserves to aid us. They are led by Egil Skalla-grimsson. The momentum has changed with the Scottas on the back foot. From the brink of fleeing, we now overwhelm our enemy and push them out of the wood to find the right flank open before us. I halt my men for a few moments, enough to regroup. I lead the charge down the slope to attack the unprotected backs of the foe engaged shield to shield with our attacking force.

We do our deadly work of rolling up the flank of the Norsemen. Under attack from two directions, their shield wall broken, panic sets in and the line breaks as men abandon their positions, fleeing. Frenzied cries from their leaders call some to their senses, and they gather in protective groups, likely ships' companies. Our superior might overwhelms these brave warriors.

I regret we lost some of our most gallant thegns, but the battlefield is slippery with the blood of the dead and wounded. The anguished consideration that I had missed the central part of the engagement and been unable to save my friends in the shield wall soon passes. I see young Edmund pursuing the Norsemen, relieved that he has survived.

Overcoming these pockets of resistance, we press on after the escaping enemy who has but one thought on his mind, to reach the safety of the ships. With this overriding intention, they flee across the ancient Roman road and past the small settlement of Storeton, which is the way they came. Their return is to be different as we soon find out. Weary from running and fighting for more than a mile, a cheer burst from their lips when they see the tall masts in the distance. This changes to groans of despair because between them and salvation lies a bog. The guides who brought them thus far are either dead or gone. How can they cross?

Now the exultance comes from the throats of our men. In dismay, many of the Norsemen wade into the bulrushes, some try to swim in the mere, others turn to fight. A hail of spears falls on those amid the reeds, many finding their targets. Our archers come at a rush, happy at last to play their part in the battle. Soon the mere is a hideous sight to the eyes of the few who make it to the other side of the bog. These weary survivors gaze helplessly on the pierced floating corpses and hear the shouted insults. While our men strip the bodies of the fallen enemy for whatever trophies they can scavenge, I see the first ship pull away from the pool into the estuary. Peer as I might, I fail to discern how many men have scrambled aboard, but later I learn some of the ships did not carry enough men to row to safety. Such is the extent of our triumph: Athelstan the King who never lost a battle approached me, his joy plain to behold. Beside him, beaming, stand two ealdormen, Osferth and Guthrum, their expressions sombre. I wonder what is amiss and ask.

"The King's cousins, Aelfwine and Athelwine—"

Guthrum left the sentence unfinished, there was no need to say more. We had lost them. The list of our dead, I later learned included Theodred and Waerstan, two bishops. Sorrowful to be deprived of valuable men, nonetheless, our consolation was great. The enemy slain counted five kings and seven jarls. Constantin, for his disloyalty, lost his son, Cellach, and my man told me I had slain the King of the Western Isles.

I hoped for lasting peace in our land as I neared my three-score winters. Slaying enemies is young man's work, and I would happily leave it to Edmund who has wrapped his arm around my weary shoulders.

"Olaf and Constantin got away," he grumbled, "but we won a great victory, did we not?"

"We did," I said, grinning at Athelstan. "After this day,

Constantin will not dare intrude into your kingdom again, and I believe Olaf's relatives in Ireland will be more than sufficient to occupy his time."

"We must bury our dead," Athelstan said.

He gave orders to our men to find his cousins who must have a burial worthy of aethelings. Hearing these words, I could not help but think of the ceorls and warriors of the fyrd whose lot was interment in a common grave. They would not join in our merry-making and boasting in the mead halls, but their sacrifice had established a whole, strong England.

27

BRUNANBURH, 937 AD

From his vantage point on a rise by a small stretch of woodland, Constantin gazed, seething with resentment, over the battlefield. The disgruntlement prominent among the many emotions he experienced before a battle, he reduced to two words: Olaf Gofraidsson. The King of Dublin had taken command of operations consigning Constantin's Scottas to the flank of the battlefield by these woods. The opportunity to set an ambush in the trees appealed to the aged king, but he found the brash, overbearing nature of his ally hard to swallow.

His armour weighed on his bowed shoulders, forced forward by the weight of the shield strapped to his back. Heavy, padded, leather gloves, designed to protect his hands from sharp blades in a battle he presumed he would not fight, made them sweat. His sons were here to wield arms for him today, and his young grandsons, mounted by his side, would not take part either. The armour necessary to cut the bold figure his men expected of him was oppressive.

Constantin sighed and brooded. How had it come to this? War, he never shirked, but it needed to serve the realm.

Wherein lay the advantage to his kingdom? His instincts in the months leading up to this confrontation were to continue with his veiled diplomatic manipulations. Had he not been successful in keeping the Wealisc away from this battlefield? The wedge driven between Athelstan and their kings had paid off. By playing on their ancient grudge against the Seax, who forced them from their homeland more than five centuries ago, meant they were not lined up against his coalition.

Why had he succumbed to the pressure of his son and the accursed Máel Coluim who coveted his throne? The answer rode next to him on horses. Grandsons: the joy of his old age! He was here today, in essence, because one of his grandsons was not. When the cur of an English king invaded his lands three years ago, a Scottas army rushed to meet him in Caithness. In that battle, Constantin's eldest son, Ildulb, had lost his firstborn son, Amlaib, to the English. Driven by hatred, Ildulb overcame his father's reluctance to wage this war. Understandable, but Constantin could not help suspect the engagement was a mistake for the Scottas. When they defeated the English as they surely would, he would take great pleasure in seeing Athelstan bend the knee to him. Either that or he would stand over his body and gloat. Revenge for the loss and dishonour Athelstan had inflicted on him with that invasion would be sweet.

Reality replaced his musings as he noted the ordered approach of the enemy. The sheer numbers of the adversary caused Constantin to frown. Peering with difficulty down to their front line, he noticed how well armed and uniform the Seax shield wall presented itself. The right flank of the enemy advanced ahead of the main army coming towards the hidden Scottas in the woods. Constantin sent a grandson with a message to alert Jarl Athils, the Viking commander King Olaf had foisted on the Scottas in the field – yet another cause for resentment. Did Olaf not have faith in his allies? Constantin understood. For his part, he trusted no-one, alliances and enmities interchanged with ease in his experience.

His clouded eyes picked out the banner of the Danish mercenaries led by one of the devious Icelandic brothers. Athelstan's plan was clear, to send the ferocious Danes to turn and roll up the Norsemen's shield wall. They would receive a warmer welcome than they bargained for. The sun rose high above the battlefield, and for the first time that day, Constantin felt the coalition could win this battle.

At a shrill whistle, the Scottas led by Athils poured out of the trees, taking the Danes by surprise. Many fell to a hail of javelins before exchanging a single blow. To his satisfaction, Constantin watched Jarl Athils hack down the Icelander, Thorolf Skallagrimsson. Ildulb, crazed with bloodlust, hewed and slaughtered all those who had the misfortune to come within the arc of his long reach. Pride swelled in Constantin's breast. The enemy's tactic had been thwarted by his superior strategy.

The smile faded from his face. What was happening at the centre? The English were pushing Olaf's shield wall backwards step by step. Constantin turned to the eldest of his grandsons.

"Your eyes are sharper than mine, do you see King Olaf?"

"There, grandfather! Cannot you make out the banner? In the midst of the shield wall? He fights like ten men. But I fear King Owain is dead. I saw him fall."

"Owain dead?"

The thought did not disturb Constantin. Owain had not pleased him for many years. The weakling did not serve him as a neighbour. Owain's son made a better prospect for the throne of Strathclyde. The reality of death struck Constantin at that moment. He murmured fervent prayers to his God that his own sons and grandsons would survive this day. On the other hand, if God deemed Máel Coluim's doom should come about here, today, he would not mourn him.

"Quick, boy," Constantin urged the sharp-sighted grandson, "ride to the back of Olaf's ranks. They will know where be the reserves. The shield wall will not hold much longer; the men held back must be deployed. Go! Deliver this message and return at once. You are too young to fight in there."

The only explanation of why Olaf, occupied with the battle, had not called in his reserves must be that he had no vision of the larger picture. When a man fought for his life, there was no time to gaze around. Constantin understood this well from his experience of the horror of fighting in the front line. Half-blinded by blood, slithering on mud, stepping over or upon dead or dying men while trying to fend off and deliver crushing blows: the shield wall was Hell on Earth.

"Good boy!" he murmured at the sight of the Norse reserves pouring into the fight. He strained to pick out his grandson riding back towards him. Ha! There! What a relief!

"You may well have saved the day for us, boy." He rewarded his grandson with a smile for the errand well executed. "See, our centre holds!"

Although it was a fact, Constantin worried. The well-equipped English were fighting so fiercely, and for sure Athelstan would have reserves he had not yet deployed. Olaf's army now held its own but, a crucial difference, with all his men in action.

Another Icelandic banner advancing up the hill! Constantin scowled. The surviving Skallagrimsson come to avenge his brother. Ildulb would make sure he met the same end as Thorolf. He sent his grandson to warn his men of the impending engagement.

This time, no surprise sprung from the trees. The Danes were ready with shields raised so the javelins had little success. Ferocious fighters, they formed into a wedge and pressed in among the Scottas. Constantin caught his breath and gazed on in anxiety as the enemy formation drove into his men. The slaughter was atrocious. Jarl Egil, blinded by grief and driven by revenge for his brother, had gone berserk and no-one contrasted him. Constantin feared for Ildulb. The Danes won the skirmish when the enraged Egil struck down Jarl Athils.

What now? Would he be forced to flee with his grandsons? No! Egil was recalling his men from the trees. They would not pursue the routed Scottas. Ah, his plan was clear! Having destroyed the Scottas resistance, he would now lead his men back behind the exposed rear of the Norse army. Disaster! But what could he, Constantin, do? He would not risk the life of a grandson in an attempt to warn the Norsemen nor would he ride down himself. He meant to stay alive; his people in Alba needed him.

Before it occurred, Constantin tasted defeat bitter as wormwood and the knowledge it would come because of the failure of the Scottas to hold the flank stuck in his craw. His reflections ended with the appearance of a figure from Hell. Tall, covered in blood, and mud-spattered, the apparition staggered towards him.

"Father! We must warn Olaf!"

"Ildulb! Thank God you're alive!"

"Give me your horse!" he shouted at his youngest son, hauling the poor lad to the ground. In a trice, he leapt astride the restive creature and galloped to the battle waxing fierce below. Too late! The Danes of Egil created a gap in the shield wall, and the English poured through to wreak havoc. The day was lost. Constantin stared aghast at the fresh English reserves descending into the affray like a pack of wolves to set upon a wounded prey. Time to flee!

"To the ships!" Constantin yelled at his grandsons. "Follow me!"

The dismal ride downhill carried them back to a village not far from the battlefield. There, Constantin found men running in frantic haste to save themselves. Could he blame them for this failure? He could not. The English pursued them, striking at their exposed backs. Constantin would have done the same in victory with the situation reversed. He urged his horse on, escape for him and his grandsons facilitated because the English were without their horses tethered at the far side of the battlefield. A solitary black-fletched arrow whistled past him too close for his liking. He spurred his steed to greater pace.

Constantin wondered whether Ildulb would survive the day. In his battle rage, his son insisted on returning to the fray when otherwise he might have escaped. A man did not reason well in the heat of battle, Constantin reflected. He gave thanks to the Lord for their horses at the sight of masts bobbing in the distance, but water stretched between the ships and them. The disaster worsened by the minute. They would ride around the mere, but what of the men fleeing from the battlefield? The swamp was nothing less than a mortal trap.

Constantin groaned but urged his mount around the obstacle, onward to safety. The extent of the defeat drove home as he rode. Apart from the gnawing fear he might lose his eldest son, Constantin reflected on the other implications of the defeat. Athelstan had completed the work begun by his grandfather, Alfred: he had united all the former Anglo-Saxon kingdoms under the Dragon of West Seax; forced the Strathclyde British and the Scots into vassalage; and in the process, turned back yet another attempt by Scandinavian forces to assert control of Northanhymbre. A good day's work by the young upstart! Constantin would escape to Alba to lick his wounds but what about the enduring effects of these losses today? Would his people blame his arrogance for the defeat? Constantin turned in his saddle to look back. The light began to fade; at this time of year the days were short and this one had flown by. What he could see of the orange-flecked sunset, he glimpsed through a black lace of wheeling carrion.

28

WINTAN-CAESTRE, NOVEMBER 937 AD

We rode towards the gates of Wintan-caestre, the rump of a victorious army. Our slow procession from Brunanburh, shedding first the men of the local fyrds to heartfelt salutations and, later, the warriors of Mierce. Each man came home to a hero's welcome. At last, our turn had come, and the first glimpse of the gate tower decked in red and gold ribbons promised well. Those colours with pride we bore, emblazoned on our shields.

The gates swung back to admit us to the cheering populace. Women waved bunches of marigolds mixed with crimson flowers. I'm no expert on flowers but they were red. Our horses, in desperate need of water and rest, parted the crowd before them and became restive when the flowers flew through the air over their heads. The population of the town doubled for the day. I guessed the nearby villages contained animals and those old men and women too weak to make the effort to cheer our reentry.

Of course, that was the significance of this event: while King Athelstan reigned, no-one needed fear leaving their homes and possessions. He was strong. No Dane nor outlaw war-band would dare torch a man's home or steal his beasts and crops, for Athelstan's wrath was not to be incurred. The people, *his* folk, loved him for it.

We left our horses and embraced our worthy comrades. We longed to be relieved of our armour and weapons that had served us so well to relapse into comfort and routine. My thoughts dwelt on my estates in Kent. Absent for years, I experienced a momentary pang of homesickness. It was hard for me to separate thoughts of home from those about my father and sister. How proud would they have been amid the jostling, cheering crowd today! *Breath Stealer* had never let me down and done more than its previous owner, my sire, would have hoped when he consigned it to me. These were my thoughts as I hung the belt and scabbard on my bedhead.

I resolved to return to Sondwic as soon as possible, with my King's permission. First, we needed to celebrate our glorious victory in the traditional manner. Athelstan commanded a feast for our ealdormen, thegns, and warriors who had fought by Bruna's watchtower. The men expected nothing less of him.

We gathered in the mead hall while, outside, the November rain thrashed the thatched roofs of the town and turned the ground into a quagmire under the feet. Inside, a crackling fire roared in the hearth in the centre of the great space, the flames casting flickering shadows on the wooden walls and woollen hangings. The clamour of happy and raucous voices subsided as the King, beside me at the high table, rose to his feet. He chose to wear a discreet gold ringlet instead of his bejewelled crown. Who could blame him? He must have been as weary as the rest of us after the journey. If he was, he made light of it in his voice. With a rustle of red silk, he lifted his drinking horn high.

"Brothers of Brunanburh," he opened to a shuffle of

nudges, winks, and general approbation, "a toast to those who fought beside us and cannot be here." He did not mean the comrades who left us on the journey down England, but those buried on the Wirral.

As a man, the Brotherhood rose from their benches and uplifted their horns. It was the only sombre moment of the night.

Athelstan set down his drink and clapped his hands for attention.

"A surprise for you, my friends, and a well-deserved honour. In our midst this evening, while we eat and sup our fill, welcome a scop from Hwicce who will relate the tale of our great victory with music. Greet Egfrid of Bathum!"

A short, hook-nosed figure with few strands of grey hair stood to take the rowdy applause and held up a lyre for all to see. Sitting on a stool, he strummed the strings before, in a surprisingly rich voice for his age, he introduced his theme.

"Friends, you who were there on the glorious day," men exchanged nudges and cheered, "I tell how King Athelstan, he of the golden hair and iron arm, drove away the Vikings. It is a tale that will echo in the halls of our children's children and forever more. Here it is!"

The room fell silent as if he had enchanted the audience. Every man wanted to bask in the lustre of his achievement. Would the scop be able to put into words the true spirit of that day? The strumming gave way to song ennobled by the deep, sonorous tone:

Athelstan King,
Lord among Earls,
Bracelet-bestower
The King smiled and fingered his gold armlet,
And Baron of Barons,

He with his brother,
Edmund Atheling,

Athelstan put an arm around his half-brother's shoulder
and pulled the embarrassed young man closer to him.

Gaining a lifelong
Glory in battle,
Slew with the sword-edge
There by Brunanburh,
Brake the shield-wall,
Hew'd the lindenwood,
Hack'd the battleshield,

At the words 'hew'd' and 'hack'd' the men drummed their
wooden beakers on the table top creating a din that drowned
the singer's next line.

Sons of Edward with hammer'd brands.

At the ferocious glare of the scop, the warriors settled
down, enthralled to hear an account of the battle. They were
grateful to be alive to enjoy the tale and sup in the King's hall.

Theirs was a greatness
Got from their Grandsires—
Theirs that so often in
Strife with their enemies
Struck for their hoards and their hearths and their
*   homes.*
Bow'd the spoiler,
Bent the Scotsman,
Some hissed and some spat at the naming of the enemy.

Fell the shipcrews
Doom'd to the death.
All the field with blood of the fighters
Flow'd, from when first the great
Sun-star of morningtide,
Lamp of the Lord God
Lord everlasting,
Glode over earth till the glorious creature
Sank to his setting.
There lay many a man
Marr'd by the javelin,
Men of the Northland
Shot over shield.
There was the Scotsman
Weary of war.

"We wearied them all right," the King crowed to general acclaim and clapping.

We the West-Saxons,
Long as the daylight
Lasted, in companies
Troubled the track of the host that we hated,
Grimly with swords that were sharp from the grindstone,
Fiercely we hack'd at the flyers before us.
Mighty the Miercian,
Hard was his hand-play,
Sparing not any of
Those that with Olaf,
Warriors over the
Weltering waters
Borne in the bark's-bosom,
Drew to this island:

Doom'd to the death.

At this, beakers thumped on the table once more, a noise like thunder as ominous as seaxes beating upon shields before the battle.

Five young kings put asleep by the sword-stroke,
Seven strong Earls of the army of Olaf
Fell on the war-field, numberless numbers,
Shipmen and Scotsmen.
Then the Norse leader.
Dire was his need of it,
Fled to his warship
Fleeted his vessel to sea with the king in it.
Saving his life on the fallow flood.
Also the crafty one,
Constantinus,
Crept to his North again,
Hoar-headed hero!

"Cowards all!" Edmund cried in a shrill voice.

"Nay! Valiant and worthy foes," Athelstan corrected him to a roar of approval while the scop glowered around the hall, peeved at this further interruption.

Slender warrant had
He to be proud of
The welcome of war-knives—
He that was reft of his
Folk and his friends that had
Fallen in conflict,
Leaving his son too
Lost in the carnage,

Mangled to morsels,
A youngster in war!
Slender reason had
He to be glad of
The clash of the war-glaive—
Traitor and trickster
And spurner of treaties—
He nor had Olaf
With armies so broken
A reason for bragging
That they had the better
In perils of battle
On places of slaughter—
The struggle of standards,
The rush of the javelins,
The crash of the charges,
The wielding of weapons—

Every man was rapt at the wonder of the wordsmith who wrought such evocative words. The sweet sound of the lyre and the enthralling voice of the scop were the only noises to be heard.

The play that they play'd with
The children of Edward.
Then with their nail'd prows
Parted the Norsemen, a
Blood-redden'd relic of
Javelins over
The jarring breaker, the deep-sea billow,
Shaping their way toward Dyflen again,
Shamed in their souls.
Also the brethren, King and Atheling,

Each in his glory,
Went to his own in his own West-Saxonland,
Glad of the war.
Many a carcase they left to be carrion,
Many a livid one, many a sallow-skin—
Left for the white-tail'd eagle to tear it, and
Left for the horny-nibb'd raven to rend it, and
Gave to the garbaging war-hawk to gorge it, and
That grey beast, the wolf of the weald.

A man at the back of the hall stood to clap loudly thinking the song had ended. One or two others took up the applause for their companions to silence them in anger.

Never had huger
Slaughter of heroes
Slain by the sword-edge—
Such as old writers
Have writ of in histories—
Hapt in this isle, since
Up from the East hither
Saxon and Angle from
Over the broad billow
Broke into Britain with
Haughty war-workers who
Harried the Welshman, when
Earls that were lured by the
Hunger of glory gat
Hold of the land.

The cheering and applause grew deafening. King Athelstan stood arms outstretched toward the minstrel who bowed, first to his King, then in all directions to the wildly chanting, stomping warriors.

"An ale for our skald!" King Athelstan called.

To unrestrained merriment, the bemused songster was surrounded in an instant with many a beaker thrust under his nose. Everyone agreed with his neighbour that the scop had rendered their day of sacrifice and honour so well that their renown would live forever. They acclaimed him until he was pink with pleasure and giddy with ale. Some called for a repeat, but the poor minstrel wisely refused. How could he surpass his first rendition? Besides, the mirth and rowdiness would only increase as the night wore on until men staggered home or slid on the floor to sleep off the excesses consumed.

I turned to Athelstan. "What now, Lord?"

"Are you tired of drinking, Ecgwulf?"

"Never!" I protested. "That was not my meaning."

"What then?"

"Will you march on the old rogue?"

"Constantin?"

"Ay."

"I will not; he is no longer a threat and as you can see, to rule over England as far as his borders is a sufficient task. To drive farther, to the end of his territory, is beyond our capabilities."

I nodded in what, in my over-relaxed state, was meant to be serious accord.

"True. But might it not be wise to install a more amenable ruler in his place?"

Here the superior wisdom of my nephew shone forth.

"I don't believe so. Far better the Scottas choose their own King. In that way, there is no resentment against outsiders. I know they are a warlike people, but they are no fools. We demonstrated we can defend ourselves against all comers. What I want most, Ecgwulf, is peace and prosperity."

"A worthy aim, my King. You will not object then if I return to Kent to set my house in order? I have been away too long, and truth be told, I long for quiet. I am too old for fighting."

"Bah! No-one who saw you fight at Brunanburh would agree! But even though I will miss your company, you have earned the right to retire to Kent. I will miss you. Come at once if I call, Uncle."

"I will!"

And it was settled. That night I dreamt of Kent and the sea lapping at the landing stage at Sondwic. A night of dreams for once not filled with blood and horror!"

I decided to travel to my birthplace as soon as the festivities for Christ's Mass were over, weather permitting. If snow shrouded the land, I would wait for it to melt like my desire for fighting. I only yearned for an untroubled old age by my hearth, secure in the knowledge that Athelstan reigned over England.

29

SAINT ANDREW'S MONASTERY, FIFE, 952 AD

After nine years as Abbot of Saint Andrew's Monastery, Death crept with insistence upon Constantin. His time on this Earth was nearing an end, as was the chronicle of his life. The laborious penning of episodes from his youth in Ireland, his reign over Alba, and of his exile latterly in this refuge of peace filled his days. It was this last chapter on which he now toiled, scratching his quill across the parchment.

At such a venerable age, his handwriting fell short of its former quality; the upstrokes were no longer as assured. How he blessed Brother Dunstan, who surely passed away years ago. Without his severe tutoring in Dublin and abandoned to his own devices, he would have squandered his youth and never learned to write. The old monk would have rattled Constantin's arthritic knuckles with a cane, had he been alive and present to witness the deterioration in his calligraphy.

Constantin smiled at the memory then sighed, weary of writing. It strained his eyes, and his joints, stiff from sitting, complained whenever he stood. He paused and glanced at a pile of documents he had written waiting to be bound as a book. The many sheets encompassed his three-score and thir-teen winters. How pleasing he could leave the annals of his life for posterity. The tales, he told with partiality, but let no man judge him too harshly, for the success he had achieved had been hard-gained through battle and diplomacy.

The last chapter must be concluded, and he would not heed Death's summons until this was brought to an end. The epilogue began with a flourish, he re-read...

"The date of the English King's decease is engraved on my memory. The twenty-seventh day of October 939. No surprise Athelstan cheated me of my revenge by dying prematurely. Wherever he resides, in Paradise or Hell, I hope he encounters my son Cellach and my grandson, Amlaib, both of whom departed this life due to him and his ambitions. A futile desire is ambition, as I learnt to my cost. We come to this life naked and depart it with no possessions; our memories snuff out like a spent candle. That is why I wish to leave this account.

"As for Athelstan, his empire crumbled in a matter of weeks after his passing. Amlaib, another so named, not my grandson, sailed from Dublin and seized Northanhymbre. Not content, he added to his conquest the Miercian Danelaw. How revenge on Athelstan was sweet by giving my daughter to the Viking in wedlock! This calculated move strengthened us both and weak-ened Athelstan's successor, the accursed Edmund, the youth who struck down my grandson in Caithness.

"I maintain that given my experience, I had much to offer my people and was ruling wisely when Máel Coluim forced me to choose between civil war or peaceful retirement. That was in 943. I came here unwillingly but was not prepared to shed the blood of my people or risk death to assuage my pride. God only knows I had enough of that crimson substance on my conscience after the pointless defeat at Brunanburh.

"Máel Coluim, my cousin, suffers from the vice of impatience. How else can his seizure of my throne be explained? Given the touch of madness he inherited from his father, I am lucky to while away the embers of my life unscathed. In 945 when Edmund expelled Amlaib Cuaran from Northanhymbre and then devastated Cwymry, he blinded two sons of Domnall, King of Strathclyde. That's a measure of the cruel times we live in. My sight may not be strong, but I possess it still. Thus, Máel Coluim became overlord of Strathclyde. Not satisfied with the gain, he marched with an army into Moray and slew its ruler, Cellach.

"To my satisfaction, news penetrated these walls that, in 946, a brawler stabbed King Edmund to death. I shed no tears over his demise. It also pleased me when Amlaib Cuaran returned and regained Eoforwic in 949, undoing Edmund's encroachment. This unrest enabled me to fulfil my own dream of revenge on the English. I arranged to meet Máel Coluim and persuaded him the time had come to invade England. He took little persuasion, such was his ambition. Down to the River Tees, he drove his army, taking a multitude of slaves and many herds of cattle. I can live in peace knowing I have done my utmost to discomfort my enemy to the end of my days. Man cannot find quiet by avoiding life. The latest news I have on Máel Coluim in the year of our Lord, 952 – sure to be the year of my death – is he joined with the English to fight the Norse-Gaels. I wish him well."

Constantin looked up from his reading and took his pen, dipping it into the inkwell. These would be the final words of his chronicle:

"I am glad my life is over. Farewell, reader! May God and my people judge me as a hero: heroic in behaviour, not because I won or lost battles. And yet, my sins weigh me down. Remember me in your prayers. Amen."

EPILOGUE

I, Ecgwulf Ealheresson, Ealdorman of Sondwic, sit outside my hall watching the rhythmic bobbing of a moored boat in the moonlight. I am old and find it ever harder not to slumber when in thought, relaxing in my chair. Above me, the sky is a brilliant canopy of stars. Whenever I sit back and contemplate the magnificence of the heavens, I drift into a deep reflection on my own unimportance.

Priests blather on about how God created the celestial spheres over our heads. It is all lost on me as I cannot conceive of such mechanisms. To gaze at distant constellations and planets makes me think how I wish to sit on one of them and consider our own Earth from afar. From on high, it would be but a pinpoint to my eye, a twinkling dot among others. I would look at it and murmur, *"There, that's my home! On it lived everyone I loved or knew, everyone who ever existed was there with their beliefs, joys and miseries. Saints and sinners, kings or ceorls, lovers, mothers, conquerors or raiders – all lived on the speck suspended like a mote in a beam of sunlight."*

Is not our globe a minuscule part of the sparkling mantle? I think of streams of blood spilt by warring tribes, so that they, filled with glory, can become the momentary rulers of a fraction of the tiny speck. Momentary? Ay, whereas the first white strands appear in my grey hair, I have lost them all: all those I loved. Ecgwynn, Aethelflaed, Alfred, and Athelstan – he was the last to perish and with his young death at two-score and five winters, his half-brother Edmund has taken his place.

Athelstan was different. He brought a meaning to my life. He dreamt of uniting the land to create a place of beauty and learning where men might live in peace, love and harmony. His *Perfecta Saxonia*, sadly, has not long outlived him. Already the fantasy fades, and I wake to reality. The Vikings have regained Eoforwic. In the far north, Constantin has retired to a monastery – the wisest thing he ever did. Will Athelstan's feat of fulfilling his vision ever be repeated?

I am weary and waiting to die. How better to fill my time than by gazing once more at the stars? Now, *there* is perfection!

THE END

ABOUT THE AUTHOR

I was born in Cleethorpes, Lincolnshire, UK in 1948: just one of the post-war baby boom. After attending grammar school and studying to the sound of Bob Dylan, I went to Nottingham University and studied Medieval and Modern History (Archaeology subsidiary). The subsidiary course led to one of my greatest academic achievements: tipping the soil content of a wheelbarrow from the summit of a spoil heap on an old lady hobbling past our dig. Well, I have actually done many different jobs while living in Radcliffe-on-Trent, Leamington, Glossop, the Scilly Isles, Puglia and Calabria. They include teaching English and History, managing a Day Care Centre, being a Director of a Trade Institute and teaching university students English. I even tried being a fisherman and a flower picker when I was on St. Agnes, Scilly. I have lived in Calabria since 1992 where I settled into a long-term job, for once, at the University of Calabria teaching English. No doubt my lovely Calabrian wife Maria stopped me being restless. My two kids are grown up now, but I wrote books for them when they were little. Hamish Hamilton and then Thomas Nelson published six of these in England in the 1980s. They are now out of print. I'm a granddad now, and happily his parents wisely named my grandson Dylan. I decided to take up writing again late in my career. You know when you are teaching and working as a translator you don't really have time for writing. As soon as I stopped the translation work, I resumed writing in 2014. The fruit of that decision is my first historical novel, *Die for a Dove*, an archaeological thriller, followed by *The Purple Thread* and *Wyrd of the Wolf*, published by Endeavour Press, London. Both are set in my favourite Anglo-Saxon period. Currently my third and fourth novels are available too, *Saints and Sinners* and its sequel *Mixed Blessings* set on the cusp of the eighth century in Mercia and Lindsey. A fifth *Sward and Sword* will be published in June 2019 about the great Earl Godwine. At the end of April, 2019 *Perfecta Saxonia* is published by Creativia and the same publishers will release *Ulf's Tale* at the beginning of May, 2019. Successively they will publish *Angenga*, a tale of time travel and *In the Name of the Mother*, the sequel to *Wyrd of the Wolf*. I'm now writing a ghost story, with Anglo-Saxon connections, of course!

Perfecta Saxonia
ISBN: 978-4-86747-989-6

Published by
Next Chapter
1-60-20 Minami-Otsuka
170-0005 Toshima-Ku, Tokyo
+818035793528

31st May 2021

CPSIA information can be obtained
at www.ICGtesting.com
Printed in the USA
LVHW110001150621
690249LV00002B/120

9 784867 479896